Element of Blank

Ann Harper Reed

ISBN 978-0-6151-4194-7

Element of Blank

Pain has an element of blank;
It cannot recollect
When it began, or if there were
A day when it was not.

It has no future but itself,
Its infinite realms contain
Its past, enlightened to perceive
New periods of pain.
                              -Emily Dickinson

Element of Blank

This book is dedicated with love to Sally,

who died so that we may see

prologue

The image of Sally dressed in pocketless Wranglers, soft-soled white tennis shoes, and a tight, striped T-shirt still lingers in the air. We, the town, probably wouldn't even think of her (already some of us must pause long to recall her) except that's all that flesh and blood lady is now, residue in our minds. At her funeral we stood together, a town on trial, our eyes passing over and confronting her murderer and lover. Then our eyes saw her two girls. We stood there numbed and disillusioned. And if we were careful as our blameful eyes looked over this tragedy, this coffin stuffed with youthful death, we caught a glimpse of ourselves. In that quiet moment of truth we had to admit that years of turned backs must have flashed before Sally as her face collided with the asphalt. Ancient ritual, with its darkened cave of prayer and smoke, has left it to us to resurrect her ghost. And so, right now, Sally stands outside, puffing away on a cigarette, wearing her tight clothes, her petite body shaking with laughter...and if we remember, she still breathes...if we remember, she still breathes.

book 1

emergence

Sometimes when I'm lying in my bed I can feel the Earth moving. And no, I'm not quoting Carol King lyrics here. I'm much more into disco, if you need to know. Just sometimes I'm aware I'm about to spiral right off the planet. Laying here last night in this hospital bed, the vibrations felt just like after the big quake in 1971. Those little quivering after-shocks were ten times worse than the real rocking, buckling quake, because I couldn't tell if they were real or just something my skin was imagining. One time, in the darkness of the movie theater, a whole crowd of us sat, uncertain if we should react. Finally someone kind of yelped and trotted up the aisle into the light of the lobby. And we all sat there (I was just a kid); the shaking unending, but soft. I wanted to leave, but my dad held my hand. He wouldn't let me go. With his hand over mine, I felt safe, almost rooted into the ground and everything seemed okay. With David holding me it's the same. This whole time, in spite of everything, part of me has always felt David holding my hand.

It wasn't like this perfect thing with David all the time. I mean I guess that's a little obvious. But it wasn't like I never had doubts or questions – even back when things were pretty good all the time. But I guess it's just hard to tell this story. I get so caught up in the memory, you know, that I forget to talk about him yelling at me in front of his friends in his uncle's garage while everybody was stoned and playing dominoes, because he thought I had insulted him, or grabbing me to show he was angry. You know – stuff like that. But it's strange because it doesn't have any place with the other things I'm talking about; like the fighting was part of someone else's relationship.

But I did find myself questioning our relationship. I couldn't help but wonder if there was a little truth to what mom had said. And I just started getting afraid I was being sucked into something I couldn't get out of. I didn't want to go to college, or anything like that, but I wanted to earn money enough to live in a real house. You know? David said he wanted that, too, but then he wouldn't want to work at the jobs he had. I don't know. He was kind of exhausted by work. And whenever I would say something, or suggest something, that was usually when he got really mean with me. And I started thinking about how much of my life I'd lost when I became David's girlfriend, instead of staying just Sally. I considered maybe a different boyfriend would be able to give me the things I needed. I thought about how Natalie and I never hung out any more, because it made David mad (and Natalie got mad at me for always hanging out with David and ignoring her). And, yeah, I just really started to recognize that I was getting pulled into something I couldn't get out of...and I decided to sort of take a break.

I broke up with David after this huge fight we had in the mall parking lot. I don't exactly remember the details, actually, but it had to do with seeing this movie, "Paradise Alley." I didn't want to go, and David had to go. Halfway through that fight I decided to break up with him. But I waited. I waited for him to drive me home, because I was afraid he'd just hit me or something if I ended things in the mall parking lot. And I was afraid, too. Not just of him, but of me making a wrong decision out of anger. That fight was so awful. Security kept driving by and asking if I was alright...asking if I needed "an escort away from the gentleman," and then driving away...and me wishing I could have left with them. David getting madder and madder, until finally I just gave in and said, "Fine. I'll do whatever makes you happy." And so we watched the movie. I don't know if you've seen "Paradise Alley" or not, but trust me you don't need to. Every thing I did, every piece of popcorn I ate, every time I breathed or crossed my legs, David interpreted as me rubbing into his face that I had been right and we were indeed watching the stupidest movie in the history of life. It would have been funny if it hadn't made David so angry. He didn't even speak to me as we walked to his motorcycle. Climbing on behind him, touching his back, felt like an electric shock of cold hatred.

It's funny how quickly you learn to adapt to something. You know? Like all my life I'd been around people like my mom and dad and Natalie. Then all of a sudden I was with David in the parking lot and we were screaming at each other, the security guards checking on us, and me plotting how I would break up with him. And it's not like I grew some gills or something and went through some terrific transformation; it's like I was instantly fluent in David's world and had been all my life. Felt more normal than living with my parents. Don't get me wrong – it makes my stomach upset to fight with David...I'd rather almost do anything. But I keep up really easily is what I'm trying to say. Maybe it's just because I love David so much, that I don't mind rolling in the dirt with him in public. I can say, "Fuck you," to the entire world when it comes to David. So even as I planned my escape, with all the dramatics of the coldness of a winter night, part of me was sure it wasn't really the end.

We got to the cul-de-sac next to my street, and I got off the bike. His anger still rising from his skin, I placed my hand on his arm. He knocked it off, and I started crying a little.

"Turn your bike off." No response. "David! Turn off your Goddamn bike." He revved it up, and then turned it off, a mean smile on his face. Then he looked up at me, in the quiet and sudden absence of the blaring motor. I began my performance, "David. You know I love you. I just can't...you know. Um, this is...I think like I should go home and then we just...you know, stop for a while."

The coldness in David's eyes made me take pause. I hadn't really finished; I wanted to speak more clearly and explain myself, but it didn't matter. He hit the starter, revved up and sped away...burning rubber on the asphalt. I was afraid he'd come back and run me down. Not that he would do anything like that, but I was afraid. That was one instant, and then the next brought another fear. The tears came up to my eyes and throat now. I recognized I'd ended something, and I filled with sadness. And also fear that I'd made the worst mistake of my life. My walk home, as each step neared that house, each step felt like a tearing inside my guts, and the softness and best of myself shredding. Tears flowing from the corners of my eyes, and I couldn't even calm down enough when I entered the house. For the first time I was glad to be invisible in a house of deaf idiots. I walked straight to my room, laid down on my bed and just let the tears flow silently.

In the morning I woke, and my chest felt heavy. Before I could even think, before my alarm had even buzzed, my eyes began dripping with tears, almost as a kind of reflex. In the night I woke once as well, from the strangeness of hearing my own sobbing. I guess I can be pretty dramatic, sometimes. In some ways, it's funny to look back at myself, flailing around, acting like it was the end of the world. But also, it really did feel like that. You know?

In that heaviness of morning heartache, I stood up and walked to the mirror. The tears increased. All my magic and light, it all seemed to have vanished. I was just plain Sally, again. And it made me so lonely to be that again. Inside a torment of emotion, and the knowledge I had to have David back, and a need for him, a panic for him, and a scream inside my throat, and a loss of breath and that need – a need that overpowered anything I could ever remember needing. And a hopeless helplessness nagging at me, because I knew David wouldn't come for me, and I couldn't go to him. I'd never experienced loss like that before, and it was awful.

I climbed into the shower and considered my options as the warm water beat against my back. Looking down at my body, I hated my familiar hips and small breasts, the hair on my arms. Don't ask me why I was thinking about my body, but I was. Saddened by my self, by the actual look of me, the options for my day came to me. "I'll go to Natalie, and we can go to the fashion center and get some food and talk; I can get caught up on my homework; I can apply to Glendale Community College; I can get a haircut and buy a new outfit with Natalie. Maybe I should think about dating someone else." I was shocked by the thought, and deeply saddened, filled with guilt.

I turned the water off and climbed out of the shower. There was this weird slowness in my movements. Not like I was actually moving slower, but like I was moving through something. As though the minutes of my life were floating in a kind of water. That's the way I'm feeling now, too. Like everything has this weird weightlessness, which only seems to make everything impossible to accomplish. I'm in the middle of something, and need to get to the other side, make my decision, but my body just takes its time moving toward that end.

But I got myself to school on time, and made it through my day. In second period I talked with Natalie. The distance between us lingered, but we pretended it wasn't there. Or at least I did. We agreed to meet after school and walk over to the Fashion Center. And I managed to float through my day all the way to sixth period. All the weightlessness, it came crashing down when I saw him. I tried to stare at my book, but all I could see were his eyes. The look of his eyes on the beach on my birthday. Tears spilled everywhere, and I just wiped them off. I didn't want anyone to notice, but I couldn't keep those stupid tears inside my eyes.

Element of Blank

Sometimes I hate being a girl, and I wished I could have learned to not cry.

So I just let the minutes pass by, wiping away those girly salt stains, trying to keep my breath muted, thinking about how much I loved David. And even with his back to me I could feel his hatred. I wanted so much to tell him, "I love you. Please don't be upset with me. I just think, maybe we need a break. But maybe we don't. I don't know. I just love you. And I'm so sorry that I hurt you. I only want you to be happy. I love you. I love you." I had no idea what was going on in that stupid class. I should have never gone, sitting in the back there with all my hurt and questions and love. At a certain point, I just tuned out. Like it was just too much, and I knew I was on the verge of getting up and doing something unforgivable, so I just shut down. Finally the bell rang. I just froze in my chair, and didn't look up until I knew he had gone.

I walked to Natalie at the lockers. She had some papers to get from Geometry, and one of her friends wanted to come along. I have to say she was pretty cool about it. She looked up at me, could see I had been crying, and said, "Next time, Joy." Joy wrinkled her brows and left all in a bunch. I was glad that Natalie was my friend; glad that she would do that for me. After Natalie got her assignment we headed to the mall. It was weird to walk in silence with her; Natalie and I'd always talked so easily with each other. I had thought about shopping, like old times, but it didn't seem fun now.

"Want to go to the Bob's Jr?" I asked.

"Yeah. Okay, sure."

So we walked in silence to the Bob's, and ordered. I got a vanilla Silver Goblet, and Natalie got a chocolate one with fries. Neither of us were really hungry. We sat down and waited for the food to come. I could hear the clanging in the kitchen and see guys wearing big white chef's hats, with hamburgers and onions sizzling on their grill. It almost felt normal, and that made me want to talk.

"So. Um, Natalie?" I waited for her to say something, but she was silent. "Is there something...I know you're upset. I don't know what...should I say something?"

"No," she said, but I could tell it was a lie. You don't know someone for four years and not know when they're pissed.

"Well, I guess I should say something, but I don't know what to say." And then I just started crying. "I'm sorry. I fucked everything up. And now you're not my friend, and David thinks I hate him, and I'm not going to college, and I don't know. I'm sorry."

Natalie just watched me. Her face wasn't mad anymore, but I could tell she didn't know what to say. In my head I guessed it was because everything I'd said made sense to her. So I just kept on crying for a while. Finally the Goblets and Natalie's fries came. I wiped my tears off, and tried to eat, even though I felt like puking. We didn't really have anything to say, but at least I stopped crying and I had told her I was sorry.

She finally spoke, "I don't know, Sally. I mean you know it's not the end of the world, but we're not really like friends anymore -- are we?"

"I don't know. I thought so."

"Well, my mom and I talked a lot about you. She even said you'd be coming back and begging to be my friend. And that I should like remind you how you treated me this whole year. So I am. And I don't think it's like a good idea to be your friend if you're like only going to be my friend when David's not around."

I didn't know what to say, so I just said, "I guess. Sorry." And kept eating my ice cream, but I couldn't even taste it, there was so much sadness in my mouth. We finished, and I said, "Okay. I guess I'll just go then. Sorry." And she just let me walk away. That felt bad, because I could tell our friendship was over if she let me walk away. So I cried again, this time in the middle of the Northridge Fashion Center, and made my way through the parking lot, where it seemed like all this mess began, and walked home.

Element of Blank

During that walk I had a talk with myself, and decided I had to stop crying. I needed to make David, and even Natalie, understand what they were missing not having me around. I needed to start being the most popular girl at Nobel High -- which was impossible. Part of me knew how stupid it was to even consider, but it seemed easier than walking home knowing I didn't have a boyfriend or a best friend. I decided to get up early in the morning, and fix up as perfect as I could, do my make-up perfect and curl my hair -- wearing the cutest outfit I could find, and try to find myself some jock or something, and become popular. And I walked lighter just knowing I had a plan. A stupid plan, an impossible plan, but nonetheless I had a plan.

In the morning I woke up, and already I could tell my plan wasn't going to work. But I forged ahead and got my shower in, shaved my body just perfect -- even my arms so that hair wouldn't be so awful-looking. My skin felt smooth and I started thinking that I might be able to pull everything off. I put a towel on and looked at myself in the mirror. My skin looked pretty clear, my excitement continued. I blew my hair dry and it looked a little frizzy, but I hoped I could fix it with the curling iron. I sprayed on some of Nancy's perfume, and went into my bedroom to get an outfit. That's when everything fell apart. "I should have done this last night," I thought to myself, "Fuck."

Of course all my best clothes were in the back of my drawers because I never wore them, and they looked crumbled, almost dusty and out of fashion as I examined them. Finally I decided to wear my Farrah shirt from the night of the fall dance, with a pair of tight tan bell bottom cords, and my Cherokees. Now I needed to accessorize – I snuck into Nancy's room and looked through her jewelry and found a cool beaded necklace with a matching anklet. I threw everything on my bed and went back into the bathroom. I realized I had wasted almost all my time looking for clothes, and I needed to finish getting ready fast.

The outfit was coming together and now I just had to pull off my hair and then makeup. I put on a little light-blue eye shadow and mascara, some blush, and bubblegum lip gloss. Started curling my hair and everything I did seemed to make it worse. I sprayed on some Aqua Net to make it set, but then it looked stiff. I tried to brush it smooth. My hair felt like steel and was ripping out into the brush. Finally I had to stop. It looked way, way over worked -- like I was trying to be a country singer like Dolly Parton or something. Seeing how awful my hair looked made me realize that my make-up looked stupid, but I didn't know how to fix it. I just tried to wipe off most of the blush and the eye shadow. I promised myself it wasn't that bad. Went into my room, ironed the cords and my Farrah shirt really quick, and got dressed. I grabbed my back pack and yelled, "Bye," to my mom.

Walking to school, it felt like the first day. You know the way you feel when you first go to school at the beginning of the year, and you're wearing your new school clothes and you aren't sure who your new friends will be, or what's happened to the people you hung out with the year before, but didn't know well enough to call during summer? Well, it felt like that. It was clear out, and a morning chill wrapped around my smooth arms and ankles. I liked the way the anklet felt against my skin -- very special, and also different, new. And I liked the way the rubber heels of my shoes sounded on the sidewalk with all the birds singing, welcoming in the new day. I knew I was a big faker, and that no one would believe I was this new person, but it felt kind of good to be someone new, anyway. Even if it was just pretend.

I got to school, and people noticed me. Guys were kind of checking me out, like they hadn't seen me every morning for the past year. And some of Natalie's friends, who've never spoken to me, said "Hi," as I passed them in the hallway. My plan was working better than I had imagined possible. I was laughing because it felt good, and also because people are so stupid sometimes. The first four periods went really well. Each class made me feel better and better. It was as though I was popular.

Until lunch. At lunch I went into the bathroom and I saw the mascara had clumped under my eyes and I looked terrible. Then I just wanted to cry. Which of course didn't help at all. It's pretty funny looking back on it now – some idiot girl crying because her make-up ran, making herself look ten million times worse. But it was awful at the time. I'd thought I was doing so great, looking terrific, everybody acting like they knew me and wanted to be my friend – and instead I just looked like Bozo the Clown with Dolly Parton hair, half flat. After cleaning up in the bathroom, people coming in and looking at me, inspecting me, I got through fifth period. But I couldn't face sixth period and seeing David. I just refused to do it. Nothing seemed to be worth that humiliation. I just decided to cut. All the briskness of the morning was over, and none of the newness – that first day of school excitement – remained. So I got my things, and started walking.

I decided to accept that the despair was unending; accept that heaviness in my chest as my constant companion. And yet the spring-filled air had this really nice effect on me. Walking home, thick clouds passing over the sunlight, and the ground warm, just walking, I wasn't even thinking...sort of just existing. Birds still singing, some silly-faced lady wandering her garden, planting Petunias – all different colors – and the knees of her pants dirty. I remember thinking, "That's what I want to be when I grow up." The only thought in my mind, this peaceful idea of who I would become, and I heard his voice.

"You not gonna even look at me?" My heart panicked to hear that voice – part of me wanted to run, the other to stop, so I compromised and kept on walking. "Can't even give me five minutes of your time?" But I couldn't stop walking, my legs were moving and my head was down. I couldn't stop. I didn't want him to see me with this stupid hair and faded makeup down my eyes. In my heart I was begging him to keep up with me, but I didn't know what to say, or how to stop. I just kept thinking about the lady with dirty knees smiling in her garden, and walked forward.

"You know what? You're a fucking trip," David said while he kept following me, walking a couple feet behind, but seeming to tower over me. I walked, my head to the ground, and he followed. David followed me – and I was happy, so happy he followed. "I just come over here to show you something. Will you at least look at it? Or is that asking too much? You just gonna keep walking?" And he stopped walking, planted his feet and shouted a little, "I opened up to you – more than to anybody and that means crap to you, I guess. Poor, little, fucking rich girl." I slowed down a lot. I wanted to look at him. "Well you don't have to worry. I'm going back to New Mexico and you won't ever see me again."

I stopped, but couldn't look at him. Finally I blurted out, really quiet and my back to him,"What?"

"So now you care? Christ. This." He walked towards me. Through the corner of my eye I could see him taking out his wallet, opening it up and showing the insides.

"You know what I got in here? I ain't got fucking money – that's for sure, I ain't got a picture of my mom – or my dad – who just died, so you know. But who gives a fuck. He sure as hell doesn't. Who've I got? You. I might as well throw this piece of shit wallet away, but I don't want to. It's like that Coca cola girl – I got to keep you. I don't know why. You sure as fuck don't care."

I turned to him. Not knowing what to say, but those tears merging into my eyes, I finally looked at David: his face full of anger and the need for someone to love him.

"David," was all I could say, and my voice cracked. "Don't you know me at all? Don't you?"

He stood there watching me; neither of us knew what to do, some kind of stalemate. Then he smiled his wicked dangerous grin and asked, "Kiss me?"

I shook my head no, but I wanted to kiss him.

"Come on. You broke my heart. At least you can kiss me."

"David, I did not. I love you. You know I love you. Don't be a shit."

"No. You dumped my ass. Don't pretend otherwise. If you want to be apart – then fine. But just kiss me."

"But I don't," my voice got stuck in my throat. "I don't want that. I didn't. Christ, David, I'm sorry. I fucked up. I'm sorry – I didn't..."

"But you still won't kiss me."

I looked at him. I looked into his eyes and threw my backpack down and walked up to him, but I couldn't kiss him. I don't know why. I just couldn't.

He asked, "What?"

"Do you want me to kiss you?"

"I asked you to."

"I know, but I'm afraid."

"You love me or not?"

I nodded and pressed my body into his and kissed him. Deeply. And the darkness of that kiss – the surrender and submersions into him tasted so beautiful. And when the kiss ended I said, "I love you, David. Forever."

And he smiled. I could tell it meant everything to him. And it meant everything to me to say it. I had him back – and I wasn't ever going to let go again. Never. But, of course, I did. And, of course, he came back, too.

I don't know. It almost seems like it's a game we play. A complicated dance where he makes me do one thing, and then I make him do another, and so on, until finally we're back at the beginning. I guess that's just the way love works. And I guess that's what we're doing right now. Doing our dance.

pie town

I guess I know you can't exist in the past, but I don't know how a person lets go of it, either. How do you let go of the most magical, unexpected moment of your life? And how do you survive the memories that make you feel like you're drowning? How do you ever move far enough away from pain? And then I return to the back of his head, his leather jacket and its cheap tan and worn pockets.

There it comes: love, that fast. A big sky and clunk and groan of a slowing semi. Alone in a dead man's house, waiting. So much waiting. So many times I looked to the sun, or moon, or dusty floor and wondered my meaning, my purpose: "Am I lovable? Am I worthy of this life?" So often it felt that I should disappear, just get sucked up into the nothingness of that big, big sky with it's shadowy, cloudy light bouncing everywhere. That nothingness, that huge, blue nothingness was my only consolation standing in that loveless house. But here I go again, jumping to the end, when in reality New Mexico danced with a whole different rhythm – adulthood, Sunday lovemaking, the sound of quiet, walking around without clothes, getting stoned and yes, that great big sky.

After we got back together David asked me to move to New Mexico to live in his dead dad's house with him. I waited until graduation in May. It was a long month and a half. The two days of our separation felt like an eternity had passed, and

Element of Blank

I had a constant need for him, physically even. It was like I couldn't screw him enough. I know that sounds crass. But it really was like some kind of biological need – maybe, I know that's not true. It was just that I didn't want to lose David, again...and I didn't want to waste all the passion within me, waiting for a more appropriate time and place. It sort of fed on itself, too. Became almost like a drug – pushing the envelope, daring the world to catch us. It made being together even more exciting. We got pretty insane about it, too: doing it everywhere on campus (in a couple classrooms, the gym, in every bathroom, except the one in the principal's office and the teacher's lounge – we tried, but we never quite pulled it off), we did it in a telephone booth, a lot outdoors, even in my bedroom a couple times. We only got caught once (in the telephone booth) – and the lady was so freaked out, it only seemed funny. Poor lady, looking at David's bare ass and my thighs, let off this little yelp and hurried away. David couldn't even come, we started laughing so hard. I don't know what we were really doing in that last couple months. But I have to say it was a good time – right, wrong, or whatever.

I waited until Sunday, a couple days after graduation, to tell my parents about my leaving. I knew it would make them insane, but I didn't care. I know that sounds awful, but I wasn't living my life for them anymore, and I really didn't care what they thought. My moving to New Mexico was like the first really adult thing I'd ever done, and I didn't really give a shit what they thought. Looking back, I wish I could have cared more, but I didn't. I packed up one bag (like an idiot I thought it'd only be warm there (I thought desert: always hot) so I only packed sandals and summer clothes with one sweater), went into the living room and told Dad.

Dad in the Lazy Boy, and my suitcase in hand...David waiting down the street, "Um, Dad...I'm leaving to go to New Mexico."

He looked over at me from the T.V., and didn't even know what to say, like he was speechless and angry. "Ahhhh. No. What? No..."

And then Mom entered with her perfect hearing, "What did I hear you say?" Her voice sounded really hurt, too. That made me feel sorry for her.

"I'm not going to community college. I'm moving to New Mexico. I'm almost eighteen, and I know what I'm doing."

"No, Sally. You – you – you can't know...No -- You can't." And for once my mom didn't know what to say.

"I'll write and be in contact and stuff when I'm there. I've – I – I've got...I know what I'm doing. Don't worry about it. Really."

Mom was crying now, and that made me start to tear up a little, too. I just wanted to get on with my life, but it was scary, too. And I don't know about you, but seeing my mom cry always makes me cry.

"Sally – please. No. Let's talk about this. When did you decide to – How are you going to – who are you -- " and then through the tears she became her regular self and started really screaming at me. "No. I say absolutely not! Do YOU hear me? NO! I know what you're up to. And no! Not with that -- that -- No! Not going to happen young lady! I forbid – NO!"

And so I just watched my mom as she kept on saying "No," doing her dramatic act for the neighbors (I guess) and finally I passed right by her. She lunged for my arm and I shoved her away. The look in her eyes; we were strangers in a way I didn't know I could be with her. I could hear mom as I walked out to the street. "SALLY!! Come back here. Tom! You're just going to sit there? Stop her! Somebody stop my Sally. Somebody stop my baby! SALLY!" It was really dramatic and stupid. By the time I hit the sidewalk I only felt relief. "Thank God, I can breathe," was all I could think. David was at the corner waiting. I ran up to him. So happy, I was almost trotting and skipping to him, my smile so huge – so much the perfect scene in a movie. And it was scary as hell.

"Drive," I said, my voice excited and

breathless. I was afraid my parents would come after us. I hopped on behind David, my little suitcase between us, and he sped off. It was so exciting. I kept expecting to have my dad pull up behind us: the Station Wagon forcing David off the road – Dad's eyes all full of rage. But we made it to the freeway. And when we got to the 405, I knew I was going to New Mexico with David, and that we were going to be adults.

So we began. We buzzed down to the Ventura Freeway and picked up the 10 and were on the way to the places I only knew as names. I wanted to go to Las Vegas, but David said it was way out of our way, and that I'd like the stars in the desert sky better than Vegas anyways. But at the time I thought it was pretty much the same the whole drive once we got out of L.A. and into the desert. It just seemed to go on forever. It felt so good, though; my arms around David, and that wide everything ahead of us. I couldn't believe we'd made it. I couldn't believe how amazing it was to be there. And it just kept on coming and going, coming and going and on and on.

It got hot; the sun pounding down, and the dry wind whipping through us. And then the sun started sinking down behind us, and cooling off. But the wind kept on ripping right through us. Dry as hell, and looking everywhere around us, it felt like we could just get devoured by the land. Swallowed up, and no one to notice. I was glad I was with David, because he could protect me. Pretty much the only person in the world I could trust to keep me alive in a place like that. And it felt so good thinking those thoughts, my body pressing into his back, my nose right up in his hair.

Ever notice how some people just have all the right stuff? Like they're in the middle of a blizzard during June and they pull a warm, downy jacket and a cup of hot chocolate from out of their ass. David's one of those people, always prepared with the right shoes and clean socks, everything. But like I said I hadn't really planned very well what I'd take with me. It was almost June, but riding on a motorcycle late at night in the desert is

just plain cold – even in summer. It wasn't that bad
in Phoenix, I guess. I started noticing the difference
when we got on the 60 and started heading for Pie
Town. David had his leather jacket, and I had my
sweater – my only warm piece of clothing. And the
wind just whipped through the yarn right up into
my skin into my bones and back out the other side.
But he didn't want to stop. He had decided we'd
get there and sleep in his dad's house tonight – so
we just kept on driving. And I just held onto him,
snuggled all I could from his warmth, and we
zoomed through the desert.

When I saw a sign that said we'd entered
into New Mexico, I felt sure we must almost be
there. I kept waiting for a nice, warm, happy town
with a funky little, happy house waiting for us.
Finally we'd pass one, and then keep on going. I'd
never been on a trip that long. David was getting
pretty irritated with all my questions, so finally I
just stopped asking him. It was all so new. And I
didn't really understand the desert yet. It seemed
all the same to me, and I hadn't learned anything

about standing and looking at something – I was still just a valley girl on a ride with her boyfriend.

Finally David leaned into me as we passed Quemado, in the early dawn hours, and saw its jail with metal doors rusted open. "We're almost there, baby. 'Bout a half hour. And then I'm going to make love to you in the house -- and scare all the fucking evil away."

I kissed David, and my heart swelled up. "How great is life?" I remember asking myself. "Great beyond anything my life ever knew." And then I laughed. We kept driving, and just knowing we were almost there made the last half hour seem like two hours. My body ached from the cold (even though it was finally starting to warm up), and the vibration of the motorcycle, and the unbelievable last seventeen hours of total life-altering change. Finally we got off of 60, onto a dirt road, kicking up dust everywhere and drove onto Double Bar Road, finally stopping at the only house in sight.

It was about 5:30 am, and we were both so tired we just climbed off the bike, and landed on the bed into a deep sleep. I would have slept in a toilet at that point I was so tired. In the afternoon when we woke up (our bodies damp with sweat – even out of the covers) I felt strange to be lying in David's dad's bed...and thinking, too, about how he was dead and maybe watching us.

"David?"

"Huh?"

"You think your dad went to heaven or you think he's still here...watching us?

"Ummm," he paused thinking, and then laughed. "What the fuck I know? But you know what – bet that fucking son of a bitch is watching us. Just to get his kicks or something. Anyway no one in New Mexico really dies. Trust me on that."

"What you mean?"

"You'll see. Like they're all ghosts here. Even if they ain't dead, yet. Everybody's a ghost...just some are dead." And he laughed and pulled me into his arms.

We both fell back asleep, and I dreamed of David's dad watching us sleep in his bed, floating above us. David's dad was really kind of happy about us being there. And he smiled a lot at me. Like in the dream he just wanted to, "make sure we put everything to good use, wink, wink." When I woke up, laughing, the house was empty (David was away getting food but I didn't know where he was) – and it didn't feel so funny. The dream instantly seemed to have been a warning, and I felt really, really far from everybody, and the city, and my family, and Natalie and the shopping mall, and myself.

I walked around the house, dirt floor in half of it, red brick in the other. It had been pretty much a one room shack, and then David's dad had built onto it, but hadn't seen the point of putting a floor in, and with all the dust that came in through the walls, I guess I could understand his logic. The "windows" in the bedroom (which was part of the addition) were actually made from those sheets of thin, hard plastic, beveled and lime green and cracked. So when I awoke, an eerie green illuminated the room with bright sunlight piercing through the holes and cracks in the windows and corners of the room. I got up, bare feet against the hard earth, and wandered around the house wearing only my underwear, looking for David. The kitchen and adjoining bathroom were the original structure. Although at least fifty years old (maybe more like one hundred years old) they seemed more solid and actually had glass windows (one small one in the bathroom and a larger one in the kitchen). In the main room was a big kitchen sink, coated with dust and a few dead moths in the drain, a counter and a shelf for food, next to the sink a wood-burning stove, that must of been at least a thousand years old and a small stack of firewood next to it. In the center of the room there was a plywood table with two wine bottles covered with red candle wax on it and 3 wooden 7*up crates for chairs, and against the wall near the door a green Coleman ice chest. In the little room was a huge old fashioned white bathtub filled with dirt and rust, with a big metal bucket for carrying heated water hanging from the wall. On the opposite wall was a dusty, scratched mirror and a counter with a chipped ceramic bowl and a metal mug, next to which David had already placed his old tooth brush and yellow plastic razor. There was no running water in the house (just a big holding tank we had to pay a water tender to fill up almost once a month), no electricity, and no toilet (only the out house, which David had already warned me about).

I put my T-shirt on and walked outside to use the toilet. When I heard someone yell, "Heelllloo." I assumed it was David and turned around with a big smile. But it was the "neighbor" coming up the driveway, 15 feet away. I ran back into the house and put on a pair of shorts, my face red and humiliated. When I came back outside he introduced himself as Joe, and had just come over to talk. I excused myself briefly and went to the out house. It was hot in there, and I remembered hearing stories of snakes biting people on the ass while they sat on the toilet hole. So I stood halfway up, and peed as quick as I could (only to realize in the end that there was no toilet paper). I did my best to shake dry and pulled my shorts back on. When I exited the out house and approached him, Joe went on talking as though we were right in the middle of a conversation.

"Yeah. I knowed the man, alright. For a long, long time." He looked over at the house and chuckled. "Not much of a goddamn carpenter that's for God-damn sure! I told him, I says, 'Why you gonna tear down half that wall.' Sure as I'm standing here, I says, 'You's only gonna ruin it. Then you won't even have shit!' We laughed, but he didn't take any mind. And I guess he finished her up alright. It's different, for sure." We both laughed a little. "How long you folks plan on stayin'?"

"I don't know." I was just relieved he was ignoring the whole embarrassment of meeting me in my underwear, and was so relieved that I had at least put my T-shirt on. "We just got here last night. Or more like this morning, I guess."

"And how's Mr. David?" He asked, and I

noticed he had a certain appeal, in spite of almost being as old as my father. I think maybe it was the way he wore cowboy boots, and faded denim, and seemed so natural, and only smiled with his eyes.

"Oh -- how do you -- ?"

"David? I known him a long time. Like I says I was friends with his daddy a long time. Not many of us in Pie Town, so I figure everybody knows your old man." He paused a moment when he said that and chuckled, and let the thought pass. "Always a wild one, that kid. Well, you know what they say, apple don't fall far from the tree. And how about you? Where you from?"

"Me? Um. From California."

"I thought so. You look like a movie star."

I blushed. "Hardly."

"No, I mean that. David's a lucky kid." Tension filled a strange pause. "Well, I just wanted to...say howdy to ya. Welcome you to New Mexico...and if you --"

David's motorcycle came roaring up the driveway. He looked at Joe and then at me, got off his motorcycle and picked up the bag of groceries which had been balanced between his thighs. He walked straight for the house, turned slightly and nodded. "Joe," he said as a kind of greeting, and walked into the house.

We stood outside for a minute. Joe spoke first, looking out at the horizon, "Sure is a pretty day. You two come at just the right time. Hot and wonderful now."

"That's great. I'm glad to hear it."

"Yep. Well, I best be gettin' on my way. You two take care and if you need anything I'm just down yonder 'bout a mile. It's the house down there with the tree next to it. Can you see it?"

I looked down over the wide desert space, and in the distance I could see a green tree leaning over a modest house. "Oh yeah. I can see it."

"Well you come visiting anytime you want, young lady. Welcome," he said, as he raised his hand up in a wave.

"Bye. Thanks!"

"Bye now," and he walked back down the

driveway. I went inside and David and I made love while the groceries sat on the plywood tabletop. It felt nice to be there. Like all the possibilities of life were there, unformed, waiting for me to discover them.

David got a job on Tuesday – which was good, because we didn't have much money between us. But it also left me there in that house for days on end with nobody to talk with and nothing to do, but try to clean the rust stains out of the bathtub and keep the dust out of the house. David was working out on a ranch near Magdalena, and wouldn't come home for a week sometimes, but then he'd stay around for three or four days before he had to go back to work.

Funny though, how my days were filled up by just the simple things like bathing. Seems like when life slows down, you can't really say where your time goes, it just gets filled. Bathing really took a lot of my time. First I'd have to get the fire going, and sometimes that meant chopping wood with the hatchet David left outside for me next to the wood pile. Or sometimes I'd go out and collect sage brush and tear them out of the ground, but they made for a pretty smoky fire, which didn't quite last long enough. After I had the wood ready I would haul water with the big bucket from the holding tank and fill the two saucepans with water. Then I'd get the fire going and heat the first batch of water really hot. Carrying the pans with two dishrags, I'd pour them into the metal pail in the bathroom. Then I'd fill the saucepans again and let them get warm and take them into the bathroom. Next I'd get naked and examine my legs to determine whether they needed to get shaved or not. I'd look at my reflection in the decaying mirror, and almost meditate for a while, kind of amazed to see myself in this environment. It's funny to say, too, but I always thought I looked beautiful when I'd see my reflection in that mirror. Perhaps it was just some trick of light, but I would always take pause and look at my face and body before I climbed into the tub, and feel kind of happy with myself. Finally, I'd grab the wash cloth and put the two pans of warm water into the tub with me. Using the wash cloth I would get my skin and hair wet and put soap and shampoo on, then rinse and repeat. Then I'd condition and shave using the water in the big pail, which by then had cooled to a nice temperature. At the end any extra water I'd just pour over my head and down my back, with it's warmth caressing my skin. I've never felt cleaner than when I'd get out of that tub. But within twenty minutes it always seemed a layer of dust had settled back onto my skin and drying hair.

I'd sit outside a lot, too. My tan got dark pretty fast. I picked a place to lay, behind the bedroom window where I'd be hidden if Joe or someone other than David came up the driveway. And I'd just lay naked under the sunlight. I did that pretty much every day after my bath to dry off. Or sometimes I did it before the bath. There were lots of birds around the sage brush. A lot more than you'd think there'd be. So I'd put down the blanket and lay there on my stomach, or on my back and let the sun dance over my body. And sometimes I'd just watch the birds hopping around; looking at the red blush on one bird breast and the skunk crown of another, and the way some would insist upon perching on top of the sage brush, even though they wobbled in the breezes and couldn't reach the insects. And some had injuries. One afternoon I watched a little black bird with an injured leg – which made no difference to it – he'd just tucked the bad leg away and hopped around slowly and finally, when he'd eaten enough, burst into flight, and you couldn't see anything wrong with him at all. Looking at the bird I thought about dreams, and hopes, and how they were like flight. *If a person has dreams, anything can happen to them and they'd still have flight, they'd still have the dreams.* Watching the bird bounce around made me want to have a dream to guide me through life. And so I closed my eyes and imagined I was the bird in flight, as I lay naked under the New Mexican sun. It was an especially beautiful morning.

Afternoons were always too hot. All I would do usually was sit inside and reread magazines or lay naked on the bed and endure, as puddles of sweat gathered behind my knees and at the base of my spine. I learned to not move around a lot, to get comfortable in one spot and just let time pass. That was a kind of meditation, too. By evening, around four thirty or five I'd get up and start making dinner, and drink a coke or sometimes a beer out of the ice chest. But when David was gone for more than two days the ice chest stopped keeping the drinks cold, and I'd just drink water after that. It would take about forty minutes before I'd notice the evening cooling and it never really got cool. A dry wind would pick up, and the temperature would drop a little. All summer long there was a level of warmth, even when the lightning storms came, and the temperature never dropped much below sixty. Northridge is a little like that, too, but there I always had the air conditioning as an escape. In Pie Town there was no escape.

Element of Blank

Nearly July when Joe came back by for a visit. I was sitting in the living room (the second half of David's dad's addition to the shack), with sweat under my eyes and wet hair on my neck, painting my toe nails, when I heard Joe's truck come up the driveway. David had been gone a week, and my spirits were lifted by the appearance of a human face in the doorway.

"Hi, Joe! Come on in."

"How you holding up? Hot enough for you?"

"Yeah. I could stand a break."

"You seen the clouds today?"

"No, I don't think so."

"Well, they'll drop it down a degree or two. Beautiful. Come and see."

We walked outside in the three o'clock heat. And, for the first time, I noticed the way the light bounces over the Earth in New Mexico. I felt like I could see light and shadows from the clouds forever, it looked almost playful. It seemed to me that the sunshine and the clouds were having a game with each other. Suddenly the heat didn't bother me half as much as it had been. Joe smiled at me, and we had an understanding without speaking.

"Well, how 'bout this old timer takes you for a beer. We'll drive over to Magdalena."

"Well, sure," I said, sort of surprising myself. "But I should get back before six, because I think David's coming back tonight."

We climbed into Joe's ancient Ford truck, and wobbled down the dirt roads towards Magdalena. The bar didn't have a sign on the door, or anything to distinguish it from somebody's home, but it was packed. Felt strange to be back with people after living in the house alone for almost a month with only David. When we entered, almost total silence rang through the bar, like it was a movie or something, only the sound of the fans rotating around the horse-shoe bar. Joe knew everybody, and smiled and exchanged remarks, but it was quiet and tense. Everyone was checking me out: not like they cared if I was under-aged, and not like they thought I was a threat, just inspecting me. I sat down and Joe ordered us a couple Coors. We didn't speak much, and when I'd finished the beer I wanted to leave. Joe understood, and we got back in the truck and drove home.

David's bike was outside the house when we pulled up. He came out of the house and glared at Joe inside his truck. I thanked Joe and ran out to kiss David. David avoided my kiss, and pushed me away.

"Bye, now," said Joe as he backed out of the driveway.

The Ford wasn't even ten feet away, when David grabbed my arms and shook me. "What the fuck was that? What you and old Joe up to?"

"David?! We just went and had a beer. It was ho--"

"You what? You fuck him and then got to let the whole town know. Where'd you go?"

"Are you joking?" I paused and decided he

was serious, "I don't know. There wasn't any name on the door. It was right on Highway 60. I don't think that's what people --"

"Shut up. You're such an idiot. You have any idea how excited I was to see you? Got you all kinds of shit. And you're not even here."

"David, I'm sorry. This is a joke, right? I didn't know if you were coming back tonight."

"Well, I told you I was. I fucking told you. But your head must be fucking rattled from screwing old Joe while I'm out earning money for you to live on. Cunt."

"Fuck you," I said and slapped him in the face.

David pushed me against the wall. "Don't you ever do that to me again. Don't you ever!" And he slapped me across the face once, and then again. I was crying now. He'd never hit me before, not really.

"Stop. Please stop."

"Bet that's not what you say to old Joe, is it? He satisfy you? Huh? Does he?" David pulled me up close to him and put his hand down my pants.

"David. Knock it off. Stop it."

"No. I'll fuck you if I want to."

I started to scream and get upset. That only seemed to excite David more, and so he thrust me hard up against the wall a couple more times. I sort of withdrew into a state of hysteria and physical pain. David pulled down my shorts and panties, so they fell around my ankles and held my arms with his one hand. He yanked me down to the ground and laid on my legs, his hand still holding my arms. I'd stopped screaming now, and felt myself rigid with hatred.

After he undid his pants and pushed my thighs apart with his knees, David forced himself into me, and started talking nice. "Oh, yeah, baby. Yeah. That feels so nice. God you feel so good. Does that feel good, baby? Come on. Let it feel good." And he kissed me softly and let go of my arms, took off my shirt and kissed my breasts. In the end it wasn't that bad. I know it's hard to understand, but I just kind of made myself pretend that it had been a sex game. And that I'd been playing along. In the end it wasn't that bad.

When we got up, David dusted off my back, and we went inside. I put on my summer dress I'd been saving for him and sat on the sofa. David lit the candles in the living room and brought out the gifts. He'd bought me a Coleman camping stove with a couple propane tanks, and also a metallic heart. When he gave me the gift I started to cry, and I thanked him.

"I'm sorry I wasn't here for you, David. I just got confused. I'm here alone so much, I just get confused."

"Yeah. But that's wrong. You can't do that. You've got to remember when I'm coming home. I'm out there working, and I want you here when I get home. Understand?"

"Yeah, I understand. I didn't mean to...I'm sorry." And I kissed him.

"You know what this is, Sal?" asked David pointing at the metal heart.

"A heart?"

Element of Blank

"Yeah, but it's special. It's called a milagro. A miracle. I saw it and I had to get it for you because you are my love miracle. And so you look on it, and your prayers come true. Just like you, my Coca-cola queen."

I looked at David, and bit my lip. "I love you," I said, and kissed him.

Being alone a lot makes a person feel like they're going insane. It feels fun though, which is hard to explain, but maybe you understand. Like all of sudden I knew I could scream if I wanted to, or take off all my clothes, if I had the desire. Something in me clicked and in one instant I knew it was okay for me to be myself – to be alive and laugh. All the things I'd considered when I first saw the back of David's head, it was as though they were coming true. My mind and my thoughts were no longer confined to the importance of shopping or wearing the right outfit or needing to speak to my parents, or even thinking I could get David to notice me by wearing a certain outfit. I was thinking my own thoughts. Not really even thinking them...the whole experience felt more basic than that. For the first time in my life, because of David and this place, I was living in the moment. I was seeing the sky; I was dancing under the moonlight naked; I was making love like an adult; I was living; and I was insane. And I loved letting myself be insane; the most refreshing drink of anything I'd ever had was to shed all the bullshit I'd worn all my life in the San Fernando Valley. Sometimes it was hard to be alone out there, but mostly it felt like floating through days in a nut-ball trance all my own, free from every convention I'd ever been forced to digest.

"But David, seriously. You know I'm not sleeping with Joe. He just offered to take me into town once a week, because he knows...Well, he knows I can't get food because I don't have a car when you're working, David. And it's too far to walk. Not to mention everything would probably melt before I got back here."

David was ignoring me, drinking his beer looking out at the sunset.

"I just want to be able to have fresh food. You said last pay period you'd be working the eight day shifts all the time now. I can't keep food for eight days in an ice chest. David! You know I'm --"

"So you want to fuck the old man."

"David," I laughed. "Don't. Please." I was afraid, though, that this might turn into another ugly fight. Nothing I could say seemed to make David believe I wasn't or didn't want to be screwing Joe. I watched him for a minute, trying to pretend his whole Joe infatuation was an inside joke, and that I was finally on to him.

David smiled at me and said, "Okay. Let Joe take you into town while I'm working. Just have a nice cold beer waiting when I get home."

"See. That's what I mean. Won't that be nice? Cold beer, and milk for breakfast."

"Sure," he said, as he took a long swallow of beer and watched the rest of the sunset in silence.

It wasn't until almost a month and a half had passed before I wrote to my parents and Nancy. I didn't have much to say, left it unclear that I was with David, but I knew I had to get into contact with them. Told them I was enjoying the summer and studying birds and learning how to cook with a wood burning stove and a Coleman cooking range. I told them it was pretty rustic living, and that I was very happy. Told them to write back care of general delivery in Magdalena, since I had to go there for groceries anyway. And signed it your loving daughter, and sort of laughed to myself thinking of their reaction to that line. Thought about my mom reading it, and saying to herself, "Nancy's my loving daughter. Nancy's not in New Mexico, is she?"

About a week later I got a card from my mom with a picture of a two bunnies on it. It was blank inside except my mom's handwriting. "Your dad and I were so pleased to hear from you.

Thought this might help. Love, mom and dad."
Inside were folded two twenty dollar bills and a
fifty dollar bill. I felt bad that I thought she
wouldn't reply when she figured out it was me,
and cried as I tried to put the money in my purse.

I decided to call her, even though David
said I could only use the phone for emergencies. It
sort of felt like an emergency all of a sudden. The
phone rang about three times. My nerve became
less and less determined.

"Hello," said Dad's voice.

"Daddy?"

"Sally. How are you? Let me get your
mother." I could hear his voice yelling over the
Fonz on T.V. "Alice! Pick up the phone. Sally's
on. She'll get it in just a sec, Sal. How are you?"

"Sally?" came my mom's voice, same as it
ever was.

"Hi Mom. I just got the card. And well --"

"How are you?"

"I'm good. I'm good. You?"

"Your father and I are just fine. Nancy

sends her love."

"Is she there?"

"No, she's back at school."

"Oh. Well, I just wanted to thank you...and I really just called to say I love you," as I spoke my voice got thinner and thinner.

"We love you, too," said Dad.

"Yeah, honey."

I almost gasped, as though I'd been holding my breath. "Well, I guess that's it. I just wanted to, you know, say that. So I better go, I guess. Bye."

"Bye-bye."

I hung up. It was so strange to talk to them, all that separates us present and not present, interfering with our conversation and making it full of meaning. Like for the first time I was talking to them like people, and yet they were still Mom and Dad. I was smiling and shaking for the next couple hours after that call. Telling them I loved them, and meaning it, which I do, was maybe the best feeling I've ever had.

Element of Blank

When a person is alone in solitude, another facet of life becomes the waiting for something to pass. My main fixation was waiting for David to come home. All my activities centered around making sure I had bathed, cleaned, shopped, and cooked for David's arrival. When there was nothing else for me to do, I would think about how it would be for David to come home and kiss me and how seeing him would invoke passion like the first time in the gymnasium, or the time at the beach on my birthday. As the clouds of afternoon would build, I would fill my mind, play movies, as rich in detail as I could come to the real thing, and play them over and over. Sometimes I'd just play the part of the lover in waiting; nothing more glamorous (or more like a movie) than watching a sunset and waiting for your lover to come back home, a thin, warm breeze ruffling my hair. It's funny to look back on, because I was posing, but only the sky and the birds could see me. I guess I was watching myself, too, funny as that sounds. Usually it wasn't as good to actually see David as it had been to dream while I waited for him. But it was an enjoyable way I found to pass time, when life got too weighted down by solitude.

Sometimes, when he was home over the weekend, David would take me into Socorro for spicy New Mexican food and lots of Sopapillas with honey, with Margaritas and Mexican beer. Then all my hours of waiting would seem to pay off, and I would almost bloom in the air conditioned restaurant. I'd play the part of the happy lover in public, and both David and the crowds would approve of my devotion. Not that I didn't love David, I did. I just pretended to be somebody other than myself, with giggles and kisses and deer eyes and my hair clean and dress fresh. Sometimes it's fun to pretend you're perfect, even though you know you're not. And I liked the way David looked at me in the restaurant, very different from the look he wore when he came home from work, hot and tired and already sick of seeing my face.

Element of Blank

The cold of fall came right after the lightning storms in July and August. It sort of happened overnight. One night I was just completely cold. There were only two blankets in the house, and that really wasn't enough. In the afternoon I warmed up again, but from that night on I had to borrow David's clothes to sleep in at night. Seemed like every hole in that house was blowing cold directly into my face, fingers, ankles and toes. Every night it was the same; as soon as the sun set a chill crept into my bones. I tried to keep the fire going until right before I went to sleep, but it was too far from the bed and didn't keep me warm enough. I put on double socks and pulled myself into a ball and forced myself to sleep, only to wake exhausted and frozen in the early dawn hours. David told me I couldn't use so much fire wood, because there wouldn't be enough for winter at the rate I was going, but I didn't care. Let him stay there by himself and freeze. Of course, though, he wouldn't because he was Captain Readiness.

The second week of chill I had Joe drive me into Magdalena. I bought a couple sweaters and a pair of sweat pants from the little thrift store there, and they helped a lot, but I hate the smell of thrift store clothes (no matter how often and how much you wash them, they always smell like some old lady's sweat). I didn't mind too much, though. Felt great to sleep warm at night.

The sun was setting earlier now, too. So with my new sweaters on I decided to take an evening stroll. The cold felt brisk and nice on my face, and I was enjoying myself. Sky above, all gray and moody, acting like it might want to rain, or maybe snow. I don't want to sound like a total goof, but I just started singing "Somewhere Over the Rainbow." And then the Bee Gees, all their songs from the Saturday Night Fever Album. I was half skipping and running, just kind of beside myself with silliness, acting like I eight years old or something. I turned back and skipped and sang all the way to the driveway, and saw the candle flickering in the house, and David's bike in the driveway. My heart sank, because I knew David would be angry I hadn't made dinner.

"Hi, Honey," I said when I entered the house and saw David at the sink. He didn't reply. "I didn't know you were going to be home tonight."

"Obviously. How's Joe?"

My heart sank, and I knew anything I would say would come back at me. "Joe?"

"Yeah, the guy you were just fucking twenty minutes ago?"

"David. I was on a walk."

"Save it."

"David. I was on a walk," I approached him and tried to make eye contact.

He turned and looked at me, with little emotion in his face, and said, "You want me to leave? Because if that's what you want then I'll just fucking go." He paused and looked out the window, "I seem to remember a time when you were begging for me to take you back. Begging to have my time."

"Of course I want your time. I didn't know you'd be here. I love you."

"But if you don't want me, then I'll just be gone until you can get your skinny ass out of my house. And then it'll be good God-damn riddance. You want to go around fucking people behind my back."

I started crying, because I didn't know how to respond. I didn't know how to make David know I loved him and only him.

"You know what, what the hell am I doing? I'll just go. You can fuck whoever you want. You don't want me, fine. Fine."

"David, please, no. I love you." I tried to kiss him, but he pushed me away.

"Don't touch me with that thing. I don't know where that thing has been."

I was sobbing now. "David...David. No. I love you. I would never."

He went into the bedroom and laid on the bed. I squatted down on the kitchen floor and cried for a while. Finally I gathered myself together and started making some canned soup for us to eat. When it was ready, I walked toward the bedroom and told him quietly that dinner was ready.

I sat at the table and waited a while. After about five minutes he came and sat down, dragging the 7*up crate over the bricks. He took one look at the dinner and sighed.

"What is this crap?"

I didn't know what to reply.

"This isn't fucking dinner. Shit." He grabbed his spoon and took a slurp. "It's fucking cold. Unfuckingbelievable." And he threw the soup against the wall, all over the cooler. The bowl broke, too. I kept thinking about the broken bowl, because we only had two bowls. "You serve cold fucking soup to me. Jesus Christ you're lazy. What the hell you do all day that you can't have a real meal for me? And you're so stupid you don't even know how to cook soup." He got up and left.

I sat in the chair, and listened as his motorcycle sped off. I didn't even cry. I went and cleaned up the soup. Of course I managed to cut my finger while I picked up the shards of the bowl. I cried then. And when I was finished cleaning up I threw my soup out into the bushes under the Juniper tree. After about an hour of waiting, looking out over the dark sky, I got ready for bed.

David came back early that morning at about two. His breath stank from whiskey and beer and cigarettes and vomit and probably other things that I had no idea about.

"Hi, baby. How's my..."

I got up and helped David into bed.

"I love you, soooo....you're my baby. My coccca..."

"Be quiet. Go to sleep."

"God, I love you. You're so beautiful. So beautiful," and he started to cry.

"I love you, too. Go to sleep."

And then he was asleep. I tried to get his boots off, but I couldn't without his help. I climbed back under the covers and slept for another hour until he woke me up. He was pretty sober now, and horny.

"Baby, make me come. Please. I want you so bad. Come on."

"David, I..."

And he caressed my face and kissed me softly. I pulled my pants off. It was over pretty fast, and David was asleep within five minutes. But I was suddenly very awake, and very aware something wrong was happening in my body. I know you're not supposed to know these things, but I did know. I got up and went to the outhouse, hoping that I could just get rid of whatever was inside of me by washing myself and peeing. Outside the moon was full. As I made my way back into the house, I had the sinking feeling I was entering a nightmare, but I had no idea what that meant.

Don't think I was being a spy or something. That wasn't it at all. Truth is, I honestly was having some cravings – that was scary enough for me to just be aware of that. I knew something,

even that night when we'd had sex, I'd known –
something was different. And that was all I had
been thinking about. But I hadn't said anything to
David. It had been so strange between us anyways.
Anything was liable to set him off, and I was a little
afraid. I didn't want to tell him until I was sure,
and it'd be a couple more weeks before I could be
sure. And then he'd said he was going to be out of
town. So when I'd had Joe drive me into
Magdalena to buy groceries and I'd seen David's
bike out front of that house, I just pretended I
hadn't noticed it.

Joe went over to the bar, and I told him,
"I'm going to do my shopping." Which I was. But
I had to go back to that house first. I had to find
out what I think I knew already when we passed
by. So I just walked along the street down Main St.
across to 2nd, over to Spruce, back up to the house
with David's motorcycle in front of it. I walked
with such a strange, surreal awareness of
everything around me. All the world was
suddenly frozen still, like in the Twilight Zone.

Element of Blank

Everything motionless except me.

The door was open ajar, so I just walked up to it. I wish I would have knocked. That would have been better. But instead I just pushed it all the way open. And there was David, looking right at me, some fat Indian, who looked like a man, but later I saw she had huge boobs, was sucking on him. And I just backed away. I didn't even say anything. I just walked back down the street towards the market, almost like I was going to just do my shopping and go home. And all of a sudden I threw up right on the road, right on highway 60. I walked over, off the road and leaned down looking at the ground, sort of gagging and crying a bit. While my body calmed down and I stopped dry heaving, I contemplated my next action. And when I could, I walked to the pay phone. It was hard to dial the operator, and when I finally did it felt like more of a trance than a phone call. The operator rang, and mom picked up after a couple rings.

"Yes, I'll accept the charges." A pause and

a click.

"Mom?"

"Hello, Sally. How are you?" her voice sounded so close and far away, and loving and distant. I just listened for a second. "Sally? Are you there?"

"Um, Mom, not really. Not so good. I'm not doing really good. And I really need to come back home," my voice full of emotion, in spite of my efforts.

"Uh huh. Okay. Well, this is your home, Sally. You know that."

"Yeah...I. It's that I need to come home. And I need you to pick me up."

"Pick you up?"

"Just come to Jackson Park in Pie Town off of Highway 60. Everybody knows where that is. Just ask...it's right on the way. And I'll just be there when you come. But when do you think you'll come?"

"How far is that, Sally?"

"I don't know. A couple days anyways.

We...when I came out here we – I got here in a day. But about twenty hours or something, I guess. Just drive out to Phoenix. And then get here the next day. Is that okay?"

"Well, I guess. If you need me to come, I'll come."

"When?"

"I don't know. I should ask your father."

I started to cry a little, and she heard.

"Sally, honey, I'm coming tonight. I'll get to Phoenix tonight."

Now I was sobbing. "Thanks, Mom. Thank you. Sorry. Thanks."

"Okay. See you soon."

"Okay. See you soon, bye," but Mom had already hung up. My body was shaking, I don't know why. It didn't make any sense. Sometimes I get like that – I mean I've always been like that. And I start just being afraid. I went to the bar and had Joe drive me back to the house, and thanked him, but didn't say goodbye. I don't know why. I went into the house and just started packing. That didn't really take very long. I took the milagro David had given me, and bent it up and left it on the kitchen table for him to find it. My body felt strange, and I knew what it meant, but I just refused to think about it. And then I just waited for time to pass – just like all the other days, but different. The end was coming and it felt different to wait with the end coming and everything. I cried, and I felt angry. A couple times a car went past and I was afraid it was David. Then I was sad that David didn't come. Night did though, and so did time. It all came and passed and danced around for me and kept on its way.

I walked around the house. All the rains done now, and the air cold, but still feeling dry like the desert. I said, out loud, "I'll miss you, house, and David's dad, and you, sky, too. Thank you. I'll miss you." And then it seemed so stupid to me to be talking to the house, even though it was true. I would miss them. So I just kept walking around, as it got later and later. At about ten, I pulled the blankets off the bed and climbed onto the foam couch – I refused to sleep in the same bed David had. Alone and cold I stared at the ceiling and walls thinking about the end of waiting, and the end of silence, and seeing my mom again, and sometimes a flicker of David in that house. And I would just begin to sob when I thought of him, and with her. And then I'd be aware of this change going on in my body. I wouldn't know what to do. Then, I guess because it was too much, my mind would let me return to thinking about the shadows in the corners of the room and what I would do in the morning.

At six in the morning I was sure David's motorcycle drove by. I almost jumped up straight from my sleep. But he never came up the drive, and I don't know if I imagined it or not. There wasn't anything left for me to do, and I wasn't hungry so I couldn't eat. I took a walk, and started feeling sad to leave, again. When I walked back to the house I was afraid David would be there, and sad, too, to discover he wasn't. I tried to tell myself that he'd come looking for me, and when he saw I wasn't here went out to find me – even though I knew that was a lie. By about noon, I was pretty hungry, in spite of feeling so rotten. So I ate a peanut butter sandwich and finished off David's milk. That made me smile – to think of him in the morning ready to have his coffee and cereal, and then discovering there wasn't any milk. It was stupid, but it made me happy. I didn't want to wreck everything in the house or anything, but I did want to sabotage David somehow. Finishing off the milk made me feel a lot better.

And then time stood still. By about two thirty, I decided to walk to the park. If I walked really slow, it only took about twenty minutes to get there, but I couldn't stand to stay in the house any longer. And I didn't want David to come back and find me. I just wanted to move on. So I grabbed my suitcase and shut the door and went down the driveway and didn't look back.

I must have waited two hours on that dirt road at the park, with that stupid suitcase packed. It was so motionless out there...like everything knew I was leaving, and they felt as sad as I was. The sunlight was warm on my back, and everything hushed quiet. Finally I saw the Station Wagon on the horizon, a steady stream of dust rising from its rear. Recognized it immediately, and felt the first pang of security I'd known in a long time. By the time she reached the snag at the corner I saw Mom's face squinting ahead, scared. Then the car arrived, just like I was getting picked up from elementary school. "How was your day?" And I was back to the land of unheard answers and sitcom questions. I opened the door and put the suitcase in the back seat, and just climbed in. I closed the door, and Mom drove on.

"What were you thinking, Sally? Christ, well, where the hell is this anyway? Good Jesus. This is the middle of nowhere." She made sure to emphasize "is," as if I hadn't realized I was living beyond the edge of civilization. "What were you thinking? Good Jesus." And I couldn't say it one more time, to one more person. "You were right. Happy? You were right." But I couldn't even say it. All I could do was look out the window as all of New Mexico, all its ghosts and its great big sky zoomed past. Thinking about the thing inside me, feeding off my body – some part of me knowing David was still with me in every possible way. And just watching all the ghosts zoom past.

love

Home. Mom and Dad's home, anyway. I've never slept in a weirder state of mind than the night I returned from New Mexico and slept in my old twin bed. The drive was impossibly long. And mom looked so small, like a little old lady holding onto a gigantic steering wheel. Strange to notice how old mom had become. Her tired, wide eyes blinking as the eastbound car lights passed us, and squinting to read the signs saying 117 miles, 52 miles, 5 miles to some destination. We stopped at the Motel Six just outside Phoenix at about three in the morning. Mom didn't speak to me, and I didn't to her. There was too much and nothing to say. We got home a little after six in the evening. It all seemed so impossible to return to, and yet there I was. My drawers filled with everything, just as I had left it last summer. "Has it only been since last summer?" I remember thinking as I opened the drawers to put away my clothes the next afternoon. That seemed impossible. Part of me couldn't even be sure I'd ever left, and another part felt I could never have lived here in this teenage girl's room, with posters of John Travolta in his tight white suit and the Bee Gees on the wall. Hard to explain it, but that's the way I felt.

The night of my arrival back in Northridge the odor smelled so familiar. Around midnight I stood outside and smelled the dying lawns smell, with the Eucalyptus in the air, and the asphalt still warm and perfumy, the neighbors' sprinklers running onto the concrete driveway. Perhaps that felt the most like home – the smell of familiar suburbia. There was also the beginnings of fall in the air, the nostalgic cooling; the clean odor of new school clothes and the school supplies' smell: plastic, and book bags, and new pencils. Standing out on the front lawn I thought instantly of David and that night at our first dance, and how he picked me over everyone else. It made me happy to have a really good memory of him, helped to diminish that last image of him. That paralyzing last image of him in someone else's life. And then I felt the parasite inside me. I knew that wasn't fair to think of it that way, but I couldn't help myself. My breasts hurt from their tightness, and there was David naked with some dikey Indian. I wanted to rip off the walls, but I just went to bed, and woke up the next morning and unpacked.

Mom was in the kitchen, and I knew I didn't want to sit around home with Mom. We exchanged morning greetings, and then I left.

Walked over to the mall. I felt the emptiness of my pockets, and my disinterest in the clothes. It was pleasing to know I was different. I was changed. I still remembered the smell of a desert rainstorm, the wet hitting the sage, the desert grass and the rotting Juniper, the pine needles and the majesty of the sky. And even though I knew no one in that mall understood those things, I did. I knew it. A thankfulness filled me, and I placed a hand of warmth upon my stomach. "Hello," I said. "We're going to be okay. Even if I'm an idiot." I needed an escape. I needed to find my way to another Pie Town, but away from that hurt, too. I didn't have a plan, or anything, but I felt like I could survive – it felt good to have that much.

I sort of just hung out for a few days, taking a couple walks a day, making plans, trying to stay out of my mom's way. Finally I decided to get a job at The Orange Julius in the mall. I knew the manager from when Natalie and I would go shopping there – he had a little crush on Natalie.

Element of Blank

So I went, said "Hi" to Jack, and he remembered me, which was a relief. I filled out the application, and started the next day, the morning and afternoon shifts three days a week. The job was minimum wage, but at least I got out of the house. I have to say, though, it turned out to be a little harder than I had thought it would be. Not like it was a mind stretcher or anything, but just the way people would look at me, like I was less than them. That was really strange. Hard to look at yourself the same way after you've seen someone look down on you. A couple of Natalie's friends who were still in high school stopped by, and I felt really, really stupid. They pretended not to know me, and my hands shook as I poured their drinks from the blender – and I don't know why, but I hadn't made enough, so I had to blend a whole extra drink to fill up their cups. I could hear the impatience of their breath, and I wanted to hide. The roar of the blender, with my back to them and the shouting inside my head to run away, to hide, to do anything, but be serving Orange Julius' to

Natalie's valley girl friends. It was mainly for the baby growing inside my body, that made it more real and sad than it would have been otherwise. Very strange to look around and say to myself, this is your life now. You really can't be like them anymore – not even pretend. They left and I caught the little pretty one, Stacy, tossing an eye back in my direction and bursting into laughter. A fire burned in my throat. I got through the day, somehow, and felt shriveled up and tiny. Like I was an ant carrying around a giant house, and it was just a matter of time before the house would fall on top of me. Walking home in the warmth of autumn asphalt, I knew everyday my person, my spirit would grow smaller and smaller and the weight upon me bigger and bigger. I felt very helpless.

That night I called Natalie's house. I knew she probably would care less, but I still missed her. But she wasn't home. Her mom picked up and was really nice, her voice filled with pride for Natalie, gushing almost. She told me how much Natalie was enjoying college and was going to transfer to USC after winter break, because she'd fallen in love with some genius or jock there. And that she was doing an internship at Paramount or somewhere, being some kind of assistant, and wouldn't be home until late that night, but that she was still living at home and that I should call on the weekend. I thought about my mom talking about me on the phone, and how she'd change the subject really quick, or only talk about what Nancy was doing. When Natalie's mom asked me what I was doing, my throat swelled up.

"Nothing much. Back, you know – I lived in New Mexico for a while. I really liked it. Um. Well, please tell Natalie I said 'Hi' and I'm glad she's so happy. Take care, Mrs. Hancock. Bye." And we hung up.

The next day I was almost an hour late to work. My dread was so huge, I just couldn't get out of the house, and then I couldn't rush, but just walked real slow and enjoyed the morning. It sounds stupid, but I was really afraid to go to work. I didn't want to have to serve another person. I didn't want to ever have to look up from a submissive posture and see someone staring down at me who I used to be able to look straight in the eye; I was afraid I'd have to lower my head and be humbled by sheltered, mean-hearted, snob-headed girls.

My being late didn't seem like that big a deal, but when I was twenty minutes late on Thursday, too, Jack fired me because he said he needed "responsible people." He seemed to feel bad about firing me, though. I felt like telling him, assuring him that I was about the least responsible person I knew, and it was okay to fire me. But instead I just turned around and left. I wanted to cry, but didn't. It was too much effort to cry. With grimness all around me I just walked over the asphalt back home. I didn't tell Mom what had happened, but I think she figured it out. Nothing was said.

I washed my uniform and returned it the next day. Jack wasn't there, and I didn't even know the two girls working that day. I just handed the uniform over and the one girl took it, without really talking. Her nails were long and had decals painted on them, and suddenly I understood it was no big deal – like who cares that I got fired from Orange Julius. At least I didn't have to worry about bowing down. I didn't feel powerful, or anything, but I did feel a little happier, a little lighter, again. Moving through the air conditioned mall, and all its new clothes' smell and roasting cashews and popcorn, with hip, loud music rushing out of Judy's, reminding me of another life, my insides felt all mixed up – but happy to be done with Orange Julius and that ugly brown and orange polyester uniform. I knew baby needed me to suck up my pride and go to work anyway, but it felt good to be done with that stupid job. There'd be something else, I promised baby, even though I didn't have a clue what it would be.

Every time I'd come up with an idea, an escape, it'd just run its course. Nothing seemed to be able to get done. It's so hard to plan for the future when you don't know what to expect or what you really want. I know that sounds strange. Probably nobody has any idea what I'm talking about, but that's what those two months were for me. Full of dread and wanting to have a solution, needing a solution, and also having no idea what it could be. Wishing David was there, and glad he wasn't. I just knew I had this baby coming, and I couldn't tell my parents, and I couldn't find a job anywhere. I would wake in the morning full of panic. Like, I should know now...I should already have known a month ago. I needed a plan. But I was too hysterical to really come up with a plan. Like I said, I doubt people really know what I'm talking about. Most people have a job, and school and marriage to help guide them through life. Suddenly, after wanting to be free from all that for so long, I was trying desperately to get into it. I didn't buy into it, but I also had a baby to consider. I couldn't only think of myself now. And it takes money and time and a house and a real job, and all the stuff my parents had to raise a child. So, I would wake up every morning for two months, my hand resting on my womb, feeling the life growing (whether you're supposed to or not), and I would panic. But I tried to talk nice with the baby, when I knew no one was in the house, and let it know I wasn't mad at it anymore for coming into my life. I was actually excited to have something love me, and only me. The baby knew I wanted it. That baby and I were going to be the center of each other's universes, and I couldn't wait. Baby had to know I wanted her.

And then it happened, and I didn't need to worry in the same way. I will never forgive myself for worrying. Why was I laying around worrying when I could have been doing something? I was only afraid, but I ruined everything. It was an awful thing I did. At first I couldn't even cry. Now I can't seem to stop. Even when I can see it's for the best, that we're both better off, I want to cry. I wish...I wish. Nothing will ever look the same.

And I am so sorry, because it was my fault.

It felt like my insides were getting twisted out of me. We were going to have dinner, and the T.V. was going. I pretty much fainted with the pain. Dad drove the car to the hospital and mom sat in back with me. I could tell she didn't know what to do – couldn't even speak. Just the tense quiet and my bleeding. When we got there, Dad opened my door to get me out. But I was in too much pain and couldn't move. Dad leaned in to look at me, and there was the blood all over the seat and my legs. His face was burning red and the veins in his neck bulging, "Sally. God Damn Christ!" He spoke in an unrestrained anger, "What did you think would happen? You put God-damn diamonds in your pocket – you put enough in there and some'll stick. God, God-damn Christ!" He stood back, slamming his hand on the roof. I was crying now. Dad just paced the parking lot while mom went and got the nurse guy with the wheel chair. Then I was inside, but it was already over. So much blood...I've never seen so much blood.

     I felt so alone to be in that bed. For the first time in a long time, I was alone again. All the quiet noise, the squeak of nurses shoes in the hallway, and the wheels, and mainly the surreal silence of midnight in the hospital. I tried to tell myself the baby had made a sacrifice, because I wasn't ready to take care of it, and it knew. This was a second chance. I felt so bad I hadn't been ready for the baby. And I also knew it was a gift to both of us that it had died. Baby didn't want to come into the world and have me not knowing what to do next, alone, working in Marie Callenders. Now that was all over. And I missed David, too. Felt he was the only one in the world who could comfort me in that moment. Because we'd both lost something. A part of both of us was gone, and he could pretend he didn't care, but I knew he did. I wanted to talk to him so bad. So I did. I just called.

     The phone picked up after the first ring, "David?"

"Sally? Where are you?"

"Um," and I started to cry, "we were gonna have a baby." He was silent, listening. "But it died. We...it -- " I tried to stop crying. "I just thought you should know."

"Where are you, honey?"

"I'm at the hospital."

"Which one?"

"It doesn't matter."

There was a silence, and he said, "I love you, Sally."

And I just cried a bit and finally said, "I gotta go. Bye," and hung up. It actually felt worse after I hung up the phone. Before I'd just been listening to the silence, pretty much in control of everything. Now I was filled with all that wanting and stuff, and all the hospital quiet seemed to echo back at me. I didn't fall asleep until after the dawn.

The doctor said I might have an infection, from when the baby miscarried, and they needed to run more tests, so they told me to stay for another night as a precaution. I asked my parents, because it was up to them. And they said, "Of course." So I just laid in bed, waiting to leave and start up my real life.

Part of me knew he'd come, though. There was something in David's voice that made me sure he'd come and be there for me. I guess I didn't count on it, either. Part of me wanted it so much that I didn't let myself think that he'd come all that way just to hold my hand. As the afternoon continued, I became more sure of his arrival. It was as though the closer he came, the more certain I was of him.

At about three-thirty he arrived. He came in like some kind of animal, not sure how to approach me. His feet shifting back and forth, until finally he sat in the chair next to my bed. Neither of us spoke for the first maybe two minutes. It felt impossible to clear the silence.

"I bet you never expected to see me. Ahh this is shit." He paused. "I don't know what there is to say. I mean I can try and explain and shit. But I know that you probably can't forgive me. Right?"

He wanted me to answer, but I just let him keep on talking. "Okay. So the thing is this: I got scared. I just didn't know what to do. I got to thinking about my mom and you and my dad. It just freaked me. And so I just started, I don't know, trying to get away from you. Like I wanted to not care. I wanted to not feel anything. And there you kept on being. Every shit thing I'd do, and you'd just put up with it. So I guess I just started trying to do something worse. Hoping that you'd stop loving me. And the shit of it is, as soon as you maybe did -- I was crying. You left me and I fucking must of cried a week. Couldn't fuckin' move around that house without thinkin' I was seeing you. And for just a second I'd be happy, thinkin', "She's back. Thank fuckin' God, she's back." But then you weren't. So I tried to not care. I really, really fuckin' tried that." He laughed a little, and then his eyes filled up with tears. "Sally, I missed you so much. I don't know what to say to undo all I done. I wish there was something. I wish." He cried a little and covered his eyes.

Element of Blank

After a second, the tears gone, he continued, "You know I ain't ever gonna find somebody to love the way I love you. I guess I just needed to figure that out. And now I have. And I promise it's gonna be different. I don't know why I done those things, except I was afraid. Like I never felt for anybody – anything. And then there you are: all beautiful and open and loving me. I should of been happy, but I just didn't understand it. I should of made love to you. Instead I just fuckin' left and tried to hurt you. I don't know why. And I know you – it's up to you to forgive me. But you ain't ever gonna find somebody to love you like me. You know that. I know I'm a fucking pain in the ass, but you know that you ain't never gonna find somebody else. You know nobody in the world can love you like me. I'm already your husband. In the eyes of Nature and God, I'm your husband already. And I guess...I want you to know I know that. And I want to marry you. If you can forgive me, I want to marry you. I'm sorry the kid died. It was my fault – 'cause I was so bad to you, and hurt you in all ways. But if you want we can have other kids. Or not, too. It's all my fault. I know that. I know I done it all to myself...by hurting you. I ruined the one good thing in my life. Please forgive me, honey. Let me love you for the rest of my life? I'll take real good care of you, and we'll be happy. You know we can be."

And I think he just ran out of words because he just stopped. I knew my answer would be yes, I knew it. But I couldn't say it. Because I also knew there really would be no turning back. And I had to make sure it was the only option for me. I really can't see my life without David. Maybe if we grow up together for a few years it'll change stuff. I know he'll never be perfect or anything, but I won't either. I bet we'll still fight. That's just the way he sees relationships, because of his parents and everything he knows. And also we'll fight because that's what we do. But also I'll always love him. Maybe that's just part of the way we show our love. You know?

book 2

warmth and suffocation

To call this place, this town, small is an understatement. It stands between two great and powerful mountain ranges which cast their shadow over the narrow valley every day. It's been said that the crust of the Earth stretches out thinner in these valleys than anywhere else. That would explain the difference in gravity here...the magic of the boulders and sage brush and also the insanity and despair of the Locals. The climate of a small town is always the same, and this one is no different...stuck halfway between warmth and suffocation. People who don't live here describe it as a town on the way to somewhere else; the town with the stop light; the place an hour away from a movie theater; the spot where L.A. gets its water; the town that reminds me of the old west; the place without any decent restaurants...Mostly no one who doesn't live here can imagine living here. And so we're isolated together in this valley, stuck with each other in spite of our differences because we're linked almost in the same awkward manner of extended families...We're all Locals, tied to each other by an invisible umbilical cord that yanks at us if ever we leave this town and by chance stumble into another Local, also stretching his or her wings. It's a bit like having two thousand aunts and uncles, and in spite of their hairy noses, horse manure smell, and/or redneck disposition, you can't help but love them a little.

This town, dedicated to talking about everyone behind their backs, speaks very little about Sally. That probably has more to do with her light and the despair of her life. Private ugliness like that is bound to make people uncomfortable. At night Sally drives through the desert in her Jeep to her house at the north end of town. Her headlights reveal the front of her house, she raises her hand in recognition to her neighbor watering his lawn in the coolness of summer evenings, and then she enters her home. And every night as she passes the threshold she can anticipate violence, despair, love, solitude, struggle, drugs, anger, sex, and silence. She is right, if he's home. And on the other side of the threshold we're standing together cheering on the home team at the football field, our backs turned and our blinders applied.

In the height of the summer, temperatures reach 116 degrees on a somewhat regular basis. In spite of that, almost no one in town has a pool.

Instead we've got the high school/town pool and the many water holes located throughout the valley. The largest and most frequented being Dezi Lake because it has a restaurant ("famous" for its deep pit barbecue) and because there's enough water for motor boats and fishing in addition to swimming. The water, however, rests stagnant for stretches of time and it's not uncommon for swimmers to leave the lake violently ill from exposure or with a fish hook in the foot. Still it remains the favored place.

Sally's favorite project each summer is to get a dark, golden tan. She works at it the whole season through until her skin looks positively the color brown. On her days off from work Sally takes Kate and Andrea to the lake where they swim and she bronzes, all to their hearts' content. She carries one of those water sprayers which she squirts all over herself while she bakes and browns. Kate and Andrea jump off the dock practicing cannon balls, and play a mysterious game of hide & seek and house all wrapped into their imaginations. And the hours pass.

Sometimes David -- the girls' dad and Sally's man -- comes and joins them. He sits in the shade drinking Bud-lite or joins into the girls' games. Rather the games with David consist of him tossing Kate and Andrea (squealing and joyful) in the water, repeatedly. When he's done drinking, and done tossing the girls, he puts suntan oil on Sally with indecent, rough fingers.

"Sal -- you're gettin a little big around the hips there," says David as he traces the oil along the crease of her butt. "I won't have you turning into one of those heifers, like half the women in this town."

Sally laughs and turns over to David giving him a warm kiss. "Now baby, you know I ain't like half the women in this town...least I hope..."and she rolls back on her stomach. David eyes her with a strange intensity to burn a whole in her back, but Sally doesn't seem to notice. "David, honey can you get the girls and me a Coke...a Diet Coke for me." She turns her head on the towel to stare at

David, "Is that okay, honey?"

"Yeah."

David stares out at the lake for thirty seconds, and Sally watches him, her breath out of her lungs. Finally, he glances around and stands up, swaggering to the restaurant 10 yards away. Sally turns her head to follow him with her eyes, and when he is out of sight she stares glazed at the tree next to the restaurant. After a minute she turns her head back down and closes her eyes as the sun shines hard on her back.

Kate and Andrea come crashing out of the water, running over the rocks with small bare feet. Andrea dives down on the towel, and Kate stands, her nine-year-old body scrawny and tan.

"Mom, can we get pizza?"

With her head turned and eyes shut, "What Katie?"

"Kate -- can we get pizza?"

"I must not be hearing you right."

"What? Pizza?" After a brief pause. "May we have pizza, please?"

"Oh, you would like pizza for dinner. We'll have to ask your dad. You girls aren't drinking the water are you? You breaking out yet?"

Andrea shakes her head no, and Kate puts her hands on her hips.

"Where's Dad?"

"He's gettin us cokes."

"I'm going back in the water...you coming, Twerpy?" says Kate as she heads back across the rocks around the lake. Andrea lays tanning herself next to Sally for five minutes and then she springs up to return to the lake with Kate.

"Careful, now."

"Yeah, Mom," says Andrea as she tiptoes back to the water.

An hour passes and David still hasn't returned with anything. Sally has turned over in several tanning positions...waiting. No David. Finally she stands up and walks over the rocky sand up the cliff to the parking areas. No David...no Jeep...no way home. She returns to the tanning spot...throws herself down, rolls onto her stomach and closes her eyes. Two hours later David returns with the Jeep. They pile in together and drive to the opposite side of the town heading north beyond the graveyard to a small community on the outskirts of this outskirt town and pull into a driveway. Home.

A slap behind a closed door echoes for miles...especially in the desert where sometimes all you can hear is the air gently thrashing. Sally sits on the front porch as the long summer evening drifts into night. Kate and Andrea have gotten into bed, on their own accord...experience has taught them this discipline. David has gotten onto his Harley and taken off. Pretty sure he'll be gone a while, but also knowing the fear of his return...to finish the job...to match the bruise on her thigh with a new swollen, welt for her face, Sally strikes a match and lights her cigarette. David won't usually hurt her in the face though because it complicates both of their lives...and because he enjoys her simple prettiness. She feels that protects her. Most times. So Sally stares out at the vastness, listens to the mild hum of her neighbors watching a movie on T.V., and wonders if David will return. Taking a deep, long drag from her cigarette Sally thinks of Kate and Andrea. And this thought stays. There is an immense heaviness in the desert silence as Sally smokes her cigarette, thinking of her two girls lying in their bed -- eyes shut and ears open, waiting, fearing.

As the cigarette smoke fills the porch and trails out into the desert night, the bounty of Milky Way stars catch Sally's eye and her mind is flooded with an understanding...*Why would we be here? Infinitely tiny and ant-like on the Earth planted next to a sage brush...Why do I matter? The complications that overwhelm me...why bother pretending they are anything beyond distraction in this vast universe? Why not laugh at the littleness of pain? Pronounce yourself victor of your own dismal light and laugh. Laugh long and loud. Because and for no other reason it feels good. Laugh. Because who would guess life slices like this. Laugh because it's possible to lessen pain through enjoyment. Laugh because there is no other means to survival. Laugh because you can. Laugh because you must. Laugh because who cares. Oo lay.*

A smile, faint-hearted, stretches on Sally's lips. The cigarette comes to her lips, uncurling and uncovering her teeth, and after a final puff she crushes her smoke into the ashtray. Sally stands up and flips on the hall light, next the bathroom light, and then she opens the girls' bedroom door and turns on their light.

"Get up. Up."

"Mom," demands Kate, blurry eyed and grumpy.

"Come with me. I always think of shit like this and I never do it for you two. We always, I don't know... spend so much time fighting...Get your sandals on. Yeah, the thongs are fine. Come on."

Sally walks to the front door, Kate and Andrea wearing nightgowns and blue, plastic flip-flops follow in a daze. Sally pushes Kate and Andrea outside. "Wait. This won't work. I'll be right back, girls." Sally shuts off all the lights in the house and again joins the girls, taking each by the hand. Three small shadows, under the vastness of the starry night.

"Okay. Look up and show me the big dipper."

Kate and Andrea look at each other with wonderment.

"Don't you know? It's okay, just find the North star and you'll be able to puzzle it together. You see it?" Kate and Andrea follow Sally's finger. They see the North Star. "It's the anchor point girls. The...it's reliable...the North Star. You'll remember the star?" Kate and Andrea nod and in the darkness they stand together for what seems a long time. Starlight reflects on the hard ground and a cool night breeze dances through Kate's long nightgown. Sally lights another cigarette and exhales slowly as she looks up at the inky sky. After she crushes out her smoke, grinding it into the ground, Sally takes Andrea's hand. "So that's the big dipper. Time for bed."

Sally and the girls enter the darkened house. They fumble down the hallway to the girls' room. In the dark bedroom, the three stand together. Finally Kate climbs back into her bed. Again they stand in silence with this new configuration. Andrea's seven-year-old hand finds Sally's adult hand.

"Mom, it's my turn."

"Andrea, honey, I don't know if your Daddy's coming home..."

"He ain't. You got him good and ticked...'cause you were having a cow about the lake," interrupts Kate's voice from the bed.

Sally says nothing, but looks through the darkness in Kate's direction. Finally in a quiet voice Sally says, "People don't have cows, Kate. Only cows have cows...or actually calves. I don't want you talking like that. It makes you sound ignorant. People get upset...they get hurt...they don't have cows."

"Whatever, mom. You know what I mean."

"Kate, watch that lip. Button it. I'm tired,

but I'm not too tired...If you understand what I mean, missy."

"Sure. Just take Andrea to bed with you. He ain't coming home."

"Kate -- button it. Now. I'm not letting you be parent. Enough. Good night." Sally makes her way to Kate's bed. Bending over, she pulls Kate into her arms and kisses her forehead. "Love you, knucklehead."

Sally returns to Andrea, takes her hand and walks her into the master bedroom. Andrea piles onto the top of the double bed as Sally flips the light on. After walking around the room removing her clothes and putting on one of David's t-shirts, Sally examines the large bruise on her thigh in the light. Her eyes peering covertly from under the pillow case, Andrea studies her mother. The light flips off and Sally's body weighs onto the bed. Together they lay for several minutes, motionless. From out of the darkness the child's hand finds her mother's back; Andrea strokes Sally until her little hand falls heavy on the sheets, her young breath shallow with sleep. Sally meditates on laughter. Silence gently drifts into sleep.

hope

Breakfast is a ritual. Words are seldom spoken, and spoken only when necessary. Sally cooks, but not well, so Kate has taken to breakfast preparation on school days: oatmeal, brown sugar, milk, and sometimes raisins...toast occasionally, and on hot, hot days cold cereal, but never, never eggs (unless Sally makes them poached with soda crackers, because then they don't taste like eggs). Today after searching the refrigerator, Kate discovers there's no milk. The ritual is off to a rough start. Still dressed in her nightgown, Kate measures off the oatmeal, places it aside, pours water into the premarked pan, lights the burner, places the pan on the flame and dashes the water with salt. Andrea enters the kitchen from the bathroom, already dressed in her summer-school clothes, but with bed head and sheet wrinkles still on her face. Kate leaves the kitchen to go to the bedroom and Sally, dressed in David's oversized T-shirt, enters the kitchen, glancing over at the stove. After testing the water, Sally dumps the oatmeal into the pan. Wearing only a T-shirt and her underwear Kate reappears, rushes to the oatmeal, searches frantically for a spoon, and desperately stirs the thick oatmeal.

"It's ruined. You ruined it. I won't eat it. Ever!" proclaims Kate as she dumps the oatmeal into the sink.

"What did you...Kate." Sally looks in surprise at Kate.

Kate begins to cry. "It was too thick and gross. I couldn't eat it. And there was no milk. You don't care about us. You...you...you don't care if we eat or miss the bus or get sick or eat or sleep..."

Sally stands still and watches Kate cry. Instinctively, Andrea gets up and walks to Kate. But Kate pushes her aside and goes to the bedroom, slamming the door behind her. Breathing constricted breaths, Sally cleans the oatmeal out of the sink. Kate sobs in her bedroom. Andrea finds two granola bars and knocks on the bedroom door.

"Go away. I hate you."

"Kate...it's me."

Quietly Andrea enters the bedroom. She climbs on her own bed and looks over at Kate crying, and then up at the ceiling. Kate's sobs come in waves, slowly subsiding only to increase when a new pang of emotion hits her. A knock, followed by Sally opening the door. Kate's crying stifles...and Sally sits on the end of her bed.

"The bus'll be here soon. You've got to get yourself together, honey...I'm sorry about breakfast. Put some pants on. You'll be fine."

"I don't want to," says Kate.

"Kate, it's not a question." Sally gets up and looks through the dresser. "Here, wear these."

"I hate those."

"Then pick something better. And now. Listen...let's drive to school together...We'll stop at the AM/PM and get something to eat. But we've got to hurry or I'll be late. Alright. I'm going to give you ten minutes. But you're going to school. Don't make me leave you on the curb in your underwear."

Kate giggles at the thought of being left for the world to see her in her underwear and Andrea joins in with Kate's laughter. Sally leans over and pecks Kate on the forehead, "Love you, kid. And you, too. Nut." She playfully swats at Andrea, who giggles louder. "Hurry up, now. Bunch of nuts!" And Sally leaves to get dressed for work.

Sally's Jeep comes speeding to a stop at the AM/PM, which is right next to the elementary school. All three girls run inside and dash to their favorite spot: Sally heads to the coffee pumps, Andrea runs to the hostess cupcakes, and Kate runs to the Slurpee machine.

"Girls, get something a little more nutritious...You want some breakfast bars?"

Andrea and Kate shake their head no.

"Can we get tater tots?"asks Kate.

"Okay...I'll grab a burrito,"says Sally as she yanks out the "hot items" from under the heat lamp.

Kate and Andrea make a face at Sally's burrito.

"What? It's what the Mexicans eat. Besides how's it any nastier than a Slurpee? What flavor is blue, anyways?"

"I don't know. It's Raspberry Blue Zinger."

They walk up to the counter and while Gary

adds up the items Sally adjusts Kate's hair and tucks in Andrea's shirt tag.

"How ya?" asks Gary.

"Same old, same old."

"One thousand forty pennies."

"Ten forty," Sally counts out the money.

"Thanks, catch ya next time."

"Next time," says Sally as she helps the girls gather their items. "So you girls'll be able to make it to school from here? Take care. Take the bus home." With a kiss the girls make their way to school and Sally's in the Jeep eating her burrito, balancing her coffee and heading a mile south to the ranger station.

There's quite a collection of people who work at the forest service...pretty much the whole spectrum: the naturalists, and the rednecks (who like power tools and cutting down trees), the good ol' boys, the women who stand tall, but like to cook their men breakfast, the hairy-legged feminists, the quiet introverts who like their time alone in the mountains, the lovers of life and sky, the losers (of the local variety) -- because it's a job, people who love to laugh, people who've never laughed, and just plain independent sorts...both male and female, whose main concern is freedom of spirit. And pretty much anything in between...and sometimes a truly dark spirit who finds refuge in the mountains and in digging ditches. Mainly, though, the local gathering of forest service crew is a light and wild mix of opposites.

This year the fire crew consists of a light and easy mesh of souls, the most separate being the foreman, Stan. The foreman's a good guy...old school masculine, with an occasional ego, but he sincerely tries to be the fearless leader. His main problem rests in the fact that he's not one of the Locals. The rest of the crew are completely different -- and of a similar stuff in that they've all grown up on the same air, inside the same cradle of mountains, and amongst the same collection of insane humans.

Actually Morgan P., the lead crew isn't a

true local either...he didn't grow up on our clean water and hasn't sucked a life's worth of this valley's dust, but he understands it. And he's also a bit insane, which endears him to this group of people. Today Morgan P. has brought to work his new kitten, Crazy Kat. Named so because of its tendency to vibrate and spaz when it sees flies or other insects. Morgan P., dressed in an old T-shirt and shorts, holds the kitten over his thin knobby legs on the perch of his bowling-ball belly for all to admire. Setting the kitten on the asphalt next to the engine, Morgan P. tries to attract a fly to show how wild his cat acts. Ralph, the assistant foreman, and a sweet-tempered Mormon, starts laughing and recalling other insane times that Morgan P. has flailed his arms in the air when trying to demonstrate a point. Ralph mimics Morgan P. in this season's favorite highlight: Morgan P., sick of bugs nipping at him after a long night of tending the fire line, loses control and starts screaming: "Bastard! Bastard! Bastard!" says Ralph while flapping his arms. Jerry and Morgan P. start laughing.

This morning everyone's stretching out for a soccer game with their chief rivals and compardres, the Helitack crew (who fight fires, too, and also fly around in a helicopter). Most of the Helitack crew have already spent years on the Engine crew; the fire crew are like a bunch of young kids preparing for a clean, dirty fight with their bigger, older siblings and frantically try to interest whatever Rangers they can to help them play against the Helitack crew. And the Helitack crew is late...as usual.

Sally comes peeling into the Forest Service compound, parks on the dirt under the old Cottonwood and hops out of her Jeep with a bounce. The fire crew look up at the noise Sally's entrance makes while they stretch. While holding one of his long, jack rabbit legs Ralph smiles brightly at Sally and scratches the long scar that covers his neck and left arm.

"Weeelll, guess you thought ya might just come to work after all, Sal. Overhead been asking about you," says Ralph as he lets go of his stretch.

"Ralph...you serious?" asks Sally, instantly pale.

"Well, yeah." Ralph makes his way over to Sally.

"The girls missed the bus. God damn-it. Sorry Ralph. I didn't mean to swear..." she pauses to think, and again forgetting herself, "Aw shit."

Ralph laughs.

"Ralph?"

"Now you gotta learn Sally...don't believe everything you hear."

"A total rat...You're a total rat!!!" And Sally points her petite finger at Ralph, who continues to laugh at his humor.

Sally turns around and balances herself inside her Jeep picking up her cup of coffee. The Diesel screechings of the Helitender (the Helitack's support vehicle) pull towards the driveway. Squirming backwards out of her Jeep Sally drops her cup of coffee, which spills all over the dirt.

"Maybe I should just go home..."says Sally

solemnly. Then she looks at Ralph whose laughter has stopped and now eyes her with interest. After a quick breath Sally's face cracks into a smile.

"Ah, come on, Ralph. You gotta know me better 'an that. Like a little spilled anything ever stopped me!"

"You okay, Sal?"

"Oh, knock it off. 'Course, I'm fine!" says Sally as she averts her head to conceal the sudden emotion Ralph's concern has conjured in her.

"Okay...Becky wants your girls to come up. Maybe this weekend. Talk to you about it more later." Ralph turns and walks with the rest of the fire crews toward the high school football field behind the compound for the soccer game. "Hey you want to play? We could use you."

"Yeah, like a hole in the head. You've never seen me play -- I got at least two left feet," says Sally smiling.

"Okay," says Ralph as he walks away waving his hand without turning back around to her.

Sally bends over to pick up the spilled coffee cup. Buck pulls into the driveway, whistling loudly at Sally through his rolled down window. Startled and amused, Sally spins around, coffee cup in hand. Buck, a homegrown, handsome, blond twenty-five-year-old smiles at Sally, and parks.

"Shoulda known it was you. I'll get you fired for sexual harassment. Don't think I won't."

"What was that? I didn't hear you," says Buck as he slams the door of his government Chevy truck.

"Sexual Hair...ass...ment. Don't think, just because I could be your mother, that you can get away with that. Actually, I should just tell your mother. By the way...you're late. They're already on the field," says Sally, motioning to the football field with her head.

"No worries. Actually don't tell her...she'd be proud. Finally, her son, pursuing a cat around town." Buck smiles.

"Who you calling a cat?"

"Never mind."

"I never you mind you, ya little cub," says Sally as she passes Buck, striking him in the thigh with her hip. "Gotta go to work. Now I expect you to come by and give me a full report before you go back yonder to your quiet little base, leaving us here with the big cheeses."

"Speaking of cheese, how's Yosemite Sam?"

"Why don't you ask him? He'll be in after lunch. I'll tell him you want to talk to him."

"Aw gee, thanks. But he's a busy man...wouldn't want to take up his time...he' lives to save. If I need to burn a couple hours, ya know, and listen to some stories about...'the old days,' when the women were men, and men were whatever..." Sally and Buck laugh. "Maybe I'll drop in. They still letting him carry a gun?"

"It's the truth." Sally shakes her head with mock fear, turns around and walks toward the main office. "Only in the Forest Service."

Sally enters the main office and she's in her element. An ease overcomes her; a confidence in her own abilities. Striding past the paper cutter and the scotch tape, Sally arrives at her desk...in her office. It wasn't that long ago that Sally was given this position, head of payroll. It still conjures pride within her. The forest supervisors are checking both Ralph's and her records for further advancement up the chain of command, and then this would be her permanent position. That she's good at her job is a source of pride for Sally; she feels certain she isn't the world's best mother and she wouldn't even want to attempt to consider if she's a good mate. Here at work though, she knows she's loved and she knows whatever the task, she can tackle it.

She plops down at her desk and begins to input the data from last week's time cards. The front office is quiet; on Monday everyone's out on the field or on days off. Paul, her supervisor, takes Sundays and Mondays for his weekend. Because she has Sunday off, Monday is the one day a week when Sally is her own boss. Sally enjoys Paul...thinks he's an even-tempered, consistent man, a family man, and a nice, unsmiling, straightforward type. But she loves Mondays, because then the office feels like her temple.

In walks Morgan P. with his kitten. Confidently, he sets the fluffy striped animal on Sally's desk. "Sally, could you maybe look after this cat? Her name's Crazy Kat with a 'K'."

Sally glances at the kitten and puts a scowl on her face. She doesn't mind the company, in fact she welcomes it, but more than that, she delights in watching Morgan P. squirm. Shifting her focus back to the computer screen, Sally continues inputting data. After a pause, he begins to speak again.

"Karen's out of town today...and I didn't want to leave it by itself at home. It's just while we're doing our P.T.'s."

"I don't know. I've a lot a work to do. Do you want to get paid?"

"Stan's mad that I took Crazy Kat in. He doesn't know how I can take care of it. I promised him he wouldn't notice her for the rest of today."

"How do you expect me to get my work

done?

"Well, save my time card for last."

"I already do that."

"You already...?"

Morgan P. looks hurt and shocked. Sally finally relaxes her scowl and smiles. Morgan P. smiles gratefully.

"Shoot, you had me. Is it okay?"

"Of course. What else am I gonna do? It may surprise you...but this ain't exactly brain surgery," says Sally with a nod toward the computer screen.

"Thanks Sally!!" Morgan P. makes his way out the door and to the football field.

After inputting for two and a half hours, Sally reaches into her desk drawer, takes out a pack of cigarettes, removes two, grabs her lighter, and heads out to the back patio next to the soda machine with kitten in hand. She drops the baby cat on the ground and lets it run about its business, petitely sniffing and scratching. Puffing happily through her smokes, Sally offers warm welcomes to the people in the barracks, and sassy conversation for those with the time, keeping a sideways eye on the kitten. Dressed in their Nomex clothes and hard hats, Tina, Julie, and Jerry (three of the engine crew members) walk by with a lawn mower, a shovel and two axes.

"Where's the funeral? You all digging a grave or what?"

Their downtrodden expressions light up when the group sees Sally. Stopping in their tracks, they set down their tools, while Sally steps back and forth in the same spot, puffing away on her cigarette.

"What's up with you all? Such pathetic, sad faces!!"

"Nothing," says Julie. "Stan wants us to fix up the front...mow and stuff for the pilgrims. But he's making us wear all our safety gear. Like a lawn mower's going to leap up and strike me in the hard hat." Julie and Sally laugh.

"Hey. Heard you got Morgan P. good," says Jerry, his eyes huge behind bottle cap glasses.

"I don't know about that," says Sally. "I still got the cat."

Jerry makes his signature sound of an entire stadium cheering, "Aaaahhhh," and holds up his right arm in the sign of victory (this being something Jerry does to express his enjoyment of an event or a joke).

Sally and the other two women laugh at Jerry's lunacy and shake their heads. Jerry joins in, not quite understanding the nature of the laughter, but enjoying his ability to provoke it.

Sometimes an entire summer can pass uneventfully...days and weeks always melt together at work. Especially when the real job is to wait. Wait for something to happen. Wait for: a fire to spark, an arsonist to get bored, a tourist to ignite their motor home...and mostly wait for the lightning storms to come over the mountains. When the fire crews head up into the mountains, Sally and her assistant, Viki, stay up all night at the compound listening to the radio: waiting to hear the voices of the fire fighters working out at the line. This season has been slow; Sally rarely works past six and she doesn't miss a single weekend in the sun.

A gorgeous day in July, even at the lake, and dry heat hits about ninety degrees. The girls each get a bag of Funyuns and a Dr. Pepper, Sally drinks a Diet Coke. In the early afternoon hours the desert bugs make a loud humming, and as the day continues the bugs grow quieter and quieter until the evening cooling, when they resound again in full force. At eleven in the pre-noon the sun shines supremely crisp and Sally spray, spray, sprays water over her golden brown. The girls dive deep to the bottom of the lake filling their hands with the clay soot, which they immediately spread on each other's faces...a natural beauty mask. Two motor boats speed in circles, tracing the circumference of the lake with water skiers attached to their ends by long ropes. The lake ripples in waves as the motors cut the water, causing Kate and Andrea to imagine they are in the far away ocean, living a far away new life.

"Mom...?"

"What, Andrea?" says Sally laying on her back with her eyes closed.

"Can...I want...wonder if you, we could go on a trip? Away?"

"Now don't you start complaining, too. Did Katie want you to ask me? She send you here? Go back and play, I'll speak with her later."

"No...not really. I mean she asked. But I want to go away." Andrea sits down on Sally's towel. Her stench (the stench of the lake water) hits Sally's nose.

"What's...you...that lake is toxic. You shouldn't play in it anymore. Ya just plain stink."

"We don't get sick. No. Mom?"

"What?!"

"Can't we, please?"

"Why?"

"'Cause I want to go to a place...a place where Daddy wouldn't know where we were..."

Startled, Sally sits up, looks at Andrea and then out at the lake.

"Your Daddy loves you very much."

Sally stretches onto her back and lets her skin drink in the sun. Andrea rises and turns to the water. With a mature sadness her small feet hit heavy on the dry edge of the lake until she reaches the water, where hippo-like she sinks into the brown soup. Kate, somehow sensing a disturbance sneaks up on Andrea and dunks her. Andrea submerges from the water red faced and coughing. She slaps Kate. Kate slaps Andrea back. Andrea yanks at Kate's hair and the screaming begins. The girls fight passionately, with total abandon and ugliness until finally Sally has to yell for them to come in. On the shore they are informed that until they can behave appropriately they will not be allowed to come to the lake.

"Everyone's going to think you're white trash brats. Alright, let's go, girls. I'm not putting up with your crap today. I don't even know if we're going to the game tonight. If you can behave yourselves. Now is the time to prove whether we're going to the game or not."

Dutifully everything is gathered. Andrea and Kate march to the Jeep. Everyone stuffs into the car and they speed onto the highway. In spite of their disciplining the wind feels good whipping through the Jeep on their wet skin, and small smiles soften their sullen faces. The Jeep speeds through town. Upon arriving home, the girls hose Dezi Lake off each other and fall into a game of space aliens settling new, uncharted planets. The sun hugs the crisp edge of the mountains as the afternoon fades into evening and the hours tick by until finally it's six o'clock, an hour before the game. .

The big game. Not exactly an all-star event, this preseason football game/fund raiser pits the Varsity players against the town's former football stars. An event though, nonetheless, and most of the town will gather at the high school football field. The girls run around the house frisky in their underwear, having already bathed and powdered themselves with baby powder and Love's Baby Soft. Sally, clean and refreshed from her daily sun bake and a long nap, wears her clean pocketless Wranglers with a new T-shirt which hugs tightly to her feminine breasts.

"Girls, get some clothes on. We've got to get going."

Wearing clean terry cloth jumpers the girls run out of their room and as they gather into the Jeep a nervous energy builds...a night on the town.

The high schoolers cruise the 1.3 miles of Main Street stretching from the AM/PM to the high school at the south end of town. Tonight, it's a good fifteen cars: at least half the high school student body, considering that no one would ever cruise alone. Only one of the cruising cars plays the stereo pumping, bass thuds; the other trucks and cars are full of sexy screams, whistles, and angry laughter. The highway patrol rear their heads and pull over a truck with a bunch of girls in the back, and Rick, the driver, tells the gray haired officer (known as the Silver Fox) he didn't know the girls couldn't ride back there...and the Silver Fox, liking Rick's wholesome good looks and football jersey, says, "Okay this time son, but next time, well let's just you and me not have a next time." And the Silver Fox returns to his car, finds another hiding spot to watch the cruisers drive the loop, while the teenage girls scramble out of Rick's truck bed onto the sidewalk.

The curbs are full of European tourists, sunburnt hikers, and the adolescents that don't yet have access to cars of their own. In constant rhythm the cruising vehicles pass (the thud of the bass and then the girl chatter and wolf whistles follow) as the pedestrians make their way through the town. Sally and the girls drive slowly through the teenage traffic jam when they spot Ralph traveling the curb amongst the chaos.

"Hey there, stranger. Where you headed?" says Sally as she pulls next to Ralph.

"Hey, Sally. Hi, girls! The same place you are...the game. Had to go to the market for some snacks...Becky didn't have time to pick up the check so I had to cash it and she couldn't shop--"

"Well, don't just stand there telling me your life story. Get your behind in the back seat there."

"Yes ma'am." And with one spring of his long limbs Ralph sits inside the Jeep and Sally lurches forward into the noisy procession.

"So did you hear anything about the selection process?" inquires Ralph.

"No, but it sure's coming up soon. I can't wait. It just makes me proud to think about it. Course I may not get it...but I think I will."

"Yeah, I feel the same way."

"Ralph, they're just plain insane if they don't pick you. Course they're gonna pick you. Just a formality."

Sally drives the jeep into the forest service compound and parks. They all get out of the vehicle, and cut across the compound to the football field. The asphalt outside the fire office is still warm, but the air temperature has cooled and it smells like hot, cut grass. Everyone's excited to party and be entertained. Outside the gate separating the forest service compound from the high school, this season's new cheerleaders work on their dance moves for the half-time "show." A tinny recording of Prince's "Red Corvette" plays at a low volume from a sticker-covered boom box. Andrea stops, transfixed by the dancers' head twitchings and bouncy jumps.

"Hey, Twerpy. You want to see the game or pick your butt?" says Kate as she turns around and sees Andrea lagging behind.

"Shut up," replies Andrea under her breath as she runs to catch up to everyone else.

The bleachers are already full up. The energy level has increased. Neighbors and co-workers exchange greetings. The male parents vehemently express the need for the Varsity boys to win and their elaborate theories on football strategy, while they sip on Peppermint schnapps in tiny paper cups. Mothers find other mothers, and they discuss their children, other people's children, observations on what people in the crowd wear and finally any exciting gossip that need be exchanged.

Ralph sees Becky up in the stands waving to them while they make their way through the mass of excited young kids lingering around the fence that separates the bleachers from the track and field. While they pass through the maze of children sucking on giant Pepsis and eating hot Nachos with spicy Velveeta cheese, Kate recognizes one of the little girls from her class. They wave at each other. Finally Ralph and the girls reach their bleacher and precariously work their way up to Becky and the babies.

"I hope there's room here," says Becky with concern.

"Hi, Becky! Let's see those babies," demands Sally.

With pride Becky holds up her newest baby, only a month old, and picks up the carrier with the year-old. Sally falls into a cooing; Andrea stands back timid and fascinated; Kate glances out to see which people she knows; Ralph reaches Becky's bench and proudly grabs Sam -- the one-year-old.

"Mom, can I go down and play with my friend?" asks Kate.

"Which friend?"

"She's from my class. Her name's Jody."

"Okay...sure. But make sure you don't get underfoot."

Kate nods her head as she happily bounds down the bleacher benches to the fence.

"Andrea, have you ever touched a baby?" asks Becky.

Andrea tucks herself behind Sally.

"Now stop that. You know me. Remember you and Katie and your mom visited me at my house when I'd just had Wade. Do you remember?"

Andrea nods her head.

"Do you want to touch the baby? Come here. Let him hold your finger. Look how small his hands are."

Andrea looks at Becky and then Wade. Putting a hand on Andrea's back, Sally ushers her towards Wade. A smile forms on Andrea's face as Wade takes a hold of her shirt sleeve.

"Look at that. He likes you," says Sally winking at Becky.

Andrea turns around and smiles brightly at Sally.

"Can I hold him?"

"No, honey. You're too little. Ya might drop him," says Sally.

"She won't drop him. She's a big girl." Becky removes Wade from the baby carrier attached to her chest and hands him carefully to Andrea. "So this is the main thing. You gotta hold his head like this. You can't let his head fall, because he can't hold it up by himself yet...He's too little. You're doing great. In a few years, you're going to be my babysitter."

Andrea holds Wade and rocks him gently like a baby doll, while he looks up at her with his blurry eyes, yanking at her long blond hair. After a few minutes Wade starts to cry. Becky stretches her maternal arms out and fetches him. Instead of returning to her seat next to Sally, Andrea stays glued to Becky's side, observing Wade's every move.

The game begins with a flurry of excitement as this year's Varsity come bursting through the cheerleaders' handmade yellow paper banner labeled "MIGHTY, MIGHTY VARSITY." The announcer in the tower directly above the bleachers welcomes everyone and plugs a few of the local stores. When both teams are on the field, the announcer asks the crowd to rise for the presentation of the colors. Out come the old timer Veterans from the V.F.W. with the American flag, and on goes the record of the Star Spangled Banner. There are some who sing and others who don't, but all stand. The football players with their helmets at their side, their huge pads covered by yellow Jerseys and their hands over their hearts, bow their heads humbly like big boys. Then the announcer thanks the V.F.W. and asks the Methodist's minister to give his prayer. All the heads fall down, and the football players kneel, as the

Minister wishes for the safety of the players and all those gathered at this game. In the end, he adds that he hopes "that the best team will win. Bless you all. A-men." And so the game begins.

There is much yelling, and coaching from the sidelines, but there are smiling faces next to the red-faced screamers. The cheerleaders try to follow the game, and yell hard with their little voices. Often the crowd, both parents and high schoolers, yell at the cheerleaders to get the hell out the way: "Okay, let's move your butts there up front." "If you can't follow the game, at least let us!" "Nice ass!" "Shut already! Shut!" The girls stoically smile and bounce, while waving at their friends. The Varsity's off to an early lead, which isn't a surprise because much of the opposing team consists of washed out Varsity players who now work 9-5 and drink 3 in the afternoon to Midnight most every night, coming home with their beer bellies to watch late-night T.V. Suddenly, the crowd goes wild -- the Varsity fumbles the football allowing the "Wash-Outs" to make a touch down.

Sally yells loud advice and Ralph laughs. Andrea and Becky take the babies to get concessions. Secretly, many cheer for the Wash-Outs, glad to see toughness is always a match for youthful brawn...and the burnt-out crowd imagines itself kicking the asses of the teenage bucks out on the field. And pride is an amazing thing: by half time (in spite of the Wash-Outs' beer guts) the Varsity leads by only three points.

At half time Sally looks for Kate, and discovers her under the bleachers collecting change that has fallen from people's pockets.

"Jody and me found a humongous stink bug that kept raising its behind at us, but couldn't make a smell. And we each got about two bucks, Mom."

"Well, be careful. Glad you're having fun."

Kate returns her focus to her search. Sally walks out from behind the bleachers and looks at the crowd gathering by the concession stands. Turning away from the crowd Sally walks to the quiet, most remote corner of the field. After standing there for a few minutes, she crouches down and presses her hand into the dirt. Carefully studying her hand, tears well in Sally's eyes. When she closes her eyes, the tears trickle out over her skin. Heavy tears weighed with unadmitted hurt. And in a brief instant Sally gives a prayer: *Dear God, Thank you. I had forgotten how it feels to be free. Thank you for touch and smell and Earth and Andrea and Katie. Thank you for reminding me that I exist and that I can yell and smile and be alive...thank you for ...I don't know, everything. Thank you.* And with that Sally nods her head, lets go of the Earth in her hand, leaves the quiet corner and joins up with Ralph, Morgan P., Jerry, and Tina.

"Helicopter 626, this is Station 6, go ahead with your location," says Sally in an official voice to the radio, while she winks at Viki.

"Station 6 we are currently crossing South Fork at a heading of 120." These words are spoken with the thud of the helicopter rotor slapping against the air and the smack of Sam's (the helitack

foreman) microphone placed right up against his
lips.

"Copy that: South Fork at a heading of 120,
at 0915."

"Station 6, we have a located another fire at
this location. This in addition to the Bear Incident.
Please contact the fire crew, they should bring
overnight gear. And let Dispatch know we have
identified and located South Fork Incident. Looks
like it may be man-caused. Right next to campsite.
Please stand by for coordinates. We'll shuttle out
of the airport."

"Station 6 copies. Will inform."

"626."

Viki claps her hands together and screams.
"Finally we'll get some O.T.!! I need that money,
baby."

"I'll get the crew. You okay with the radio?
I guess this is as good a time as any for you to
learn." Viki's face turns pale and she pushes a
plump hand through her thin blond hair.
Laughing at Viki's terror, Sally waves good-bye

and hops into her jeep just as Ralph, radio in hand, sprints onto the compound's asphalt.

"Thanks for manning the radio, Sal. They're about a mile back there, along Redman. Would you mind getting 'em?" asks Ralph, a bit winded.

"It's why we're here. Viki's on the radio...make sure she answers. 'Less she's already had a seizure." Sally and Ralph laugh at the thought of Viki on the radio. Smiling, Sally pulls out the driveway toward the dump where the rest of the engine crew finish their P.T.s, hustling breathless and red-necked to get back to the base. One by one Sally collects the sweaty-faced crew and speeds back to the station.

Looking for Viki, Sally thrusts open the office door. Viki sits, her thick back toward Sally, breathing in heavy snorts, tightening her sides against her big cotton shirt as she inhales. After she turns and glances at Sally, Viki pushes away the tears on her puffy, red cheeks and smiles shyly.

"You got me!"

"What's that mean? I'm so sorry you're this upset."

"What'd you expect, ya know? Now everyone on the entire forest thinks I'm an idiot. Three times. And I still didn't get it down. It took me so long, Ralph finally comes all the way from the station just to show me he had already written everything -- the coordinates --down."

"Honey. It's okay. No one starts out knowing this stuff...and all the number stuff is hard. Besides which -- you kept asking them for the numbers. That's good. It shows you're ballsy. Mostly people would act like they had it, when they didn't. I probably would of."

"Really? It was good that I asked?"

" 'Course. It's how you'll learn. Listen to the radio different now?"

"Yeah." After thinking to herself and gaining her breath back Viki says, "Sorry about saying you're trying to humiliate me."

"You know what...I just about couldn't

humiliate anyone. My life just ain't together enough to cast stones."

Viki looks at Sally with surprise. Sally's lips tremble a little and she shakes her head to show it's more than she wants to talk about. Viki breaks into a smile and wraps her arms around Sally. Pressed hard against Viki's musty perfume and mildly damp cotton shirt, Sally at first pulls back, but then realizes that she has no option in this embrace. Viki's softness engulfs Sally. A self-conscious laugh slips from Viki when she releases Sally.

"Thanks, Viki. I needed that."

Sally walks to her desk, more empty after that embrace than if she'd just been yelled at...

old habits

Need is a many-edged word. To need...When you need just enough, people are drawn toward you, but when you need too much, people run away. Need a lover. Need a place to feel safe. Need peace. Need escape. Need to buy groceries. Need tenderness. Need to loose weight.

Need a friend. Need space. Need to excel. Need a tan. Need to be a good mother. Need to work. Need love. Need to succeed. Need to breathe. Need. Need. Need. Need.

It even sounds greedy and repulsive: Need. Like a deformed creature from out of swampy waters should be gasping it. Maybe that was Sally's biggest problem...maybe there was a deformed creature hidden within her. And although we couldn't see it, we knew instinctively to pull back until Sally returned needing less, her monster back under control...

Sally's Jeep drives up to the elementary school on an exceptionally hot afternoon (that won't really cool down for about four more hours). Under the hot sun, standing along the chain link fence, Kate and Andrea wait to board the bus. Andrea, sweat pebbles on her nose and her book bag sagging from her body, stares blankly at the abandoned kindergarten playground. A few feet away Kate talks with a friend, her heated body guided by Andrea's same resigned vacancy. And then Kate's eye catches the Jeep, with an exuberant smile she waves to Sally and pokes Andrea's arm. Annoyed, Andrea follows Kate's stare, joins in with a smile of her own, and in spite of the heat, the girls run to the Jeep.

Through a bit of difficulty the girls make their way into the car, tossing bags and books on the Jeep's floor.

"No. In back. I called shotgun. Mom! I called shotgun," says Kate as she yanks Andrea backwards out of the passenger seat.

"Knock it off," cries Andrea. "Did not. Did not. You didn't."

"Girls - get in. Now."

Andrea looks at Kate (who stares at her with defiance) and crawls humbly over the stick shift to the torn upholstery of the bench seat in back. Triumphant, Kate enters the Jeep. Sally pulls forward, and watches Andrea's sulky face in the rear view mirror.

After a brief reflection, Sally purposes a

solution. "Frosty Stop?"

Cheers from both Kate and Andrea.

"Remember the ice cream melts and you've got to have a hamburger first -- so it's shakes or no breaks. 'Cause we're getting it to go."

"Mom!" cries Kate as if some extreme torture's being practiced on her.

"Kate -- Do you want Frosty Stop?"

"Yeah – but..."

"Kate, button it." And with that final remark, the war continues in its silent form as the Jeep travels the one block to the Frosty Stop.

Quietly they file out of the vehicle, with somber faces. Kate storms ahead. Sally slows and watches through the glass door as Andrea enters. From behind the door she watches her two girls stand next to each other, tilting their heads back reading the giant hand-painted menu. With motherly awe Sally sees Andrea edge closer to her big sister, and she watches Kate let her little sister draw nearer. After a passage of time, Kate turns to the door with watchful eyes, soft...uncertain, and

Sally enters the Frosty Stop. Twenty minutes later, when the door of the Frosty Stop opens again, Sally and Andrea each hold a bag of food, while Kate carries a drink in one hand, and in the other...an ice cream cone.

Sally's kitchen is covered with fast food paper wrappers. Dinner's finished. Kate licks her sticky fingers while she reads her Judy Blume novel and Andrea stares transfixed at a rerun of "Laverne and Shirley" on channel five. Smoking out on the porch Sally looks over at her girls. While she puffs, the neighbor drives past, carefully and quickly averting his eyes from Sally. Another puff, another puff, and then a glance again at her girls.

"Katie, wash your face and get me your brush. Your hair's a rat's nest."

"Mom. I'm reading."

"Why does everything need to be a contest with you?"

"Fine!" says Kate as she slams down her

book and storms to the bathroom where she opens the door with a bang. Splashing water on her face and hands, Kate looks up at the mirror with a sour face. Grabbing a brush Kate exits the bathroom. In a flurry she lands with a huff at the floor beneath Sally's feet. Sally softly drags the brush over Kate's hair.

"Ouch!"

Laughing Sally says, "You're such a butt. Settle down -- of course it'll hurt...'cause you've got enough nests in here to house all the rats in this whole valley in your hair." Sally stops and kisses the top of Kate's head. "Katie, I'm being careful. I promise. I don't wanta hurt you."

Everyone's in bed. And everyone has an unsettled feeling. From years of practice they can sense when he is returning...just by a vibration in the air, there is an inherent knowledge of his return. Sally lays in bed wearing David's T-shirt when the Harley pulls into the driveway, causing dogs to bark throughout the stillness of the finally cool night. With dread Sally lays still for several minutes, but eventually she rises. In the other room, Kate gets out of her bed and climbs in with sleepy-headed Andrea. It is quiet now, but Kate knows their little home will soon be filled with noise. The kind of noises which reverberate echoes long after their actual vibrations have ended.

Entering from the hallway Sally sees David in the middle of the kitchen. "Hey, Baby," she says.

David ignores Sally and starts looking through the cupboards. Slamming one shut and opening the same one again. Stirring around the items on the counter and pushing pans onto the floor. Even his heavy boots are loud on the kitchen linoleum.

Sally stands at the hallway. "I've missed you, ya know. You hungry? I could...I mean we got peanut butter, baby. I'll make you a sandwich."

"That'd be great. But I got one question for you, Queenie: How the fuck you going to make me a sandwich when you ain't got bread?" His eyes return to the cupboard, "You're nothing but a lazy ass whore."

"Asshole," says Sally with an inviting laugh. David ignores her. The smile fades and a wash of worry comes over Sally's face. "Daddy I been trying so hard to be good. I'm...I want to be your good girl."

"Fuck you do. Can't even have food. What's this -- ?" David picks up the fast food wrappers from the kitchen table and thrusts them down to the ground. "You feed your girls piss food because you're too lazy to get off your fat ass. I mean just look at you."

Heavy silence fills the kitchen as Sally and David look at each other. Her eyes drop to the ground and she turns to leave the kitchen and David socks her with his fist into her buttocks. Yelping sharply, Sally spins around with violent rage in her eyes.

David smiles. "There you go. Just look at it. Maybe I aught'a knock the fat right off. You've been tryin to be good. How's that?"

"I don't know."

"Look at me!"

"David, baby. I missed you. Don't--"

David slaps Sally sharply in the mouth, and as his action registers he slams her against the wall. Crippled with rage and hurt Sally slides down the wall toward the floor. David watches her, studies her, walks up to her and grabs her hair. Threatening to punch her face he asks, "How you been good? Tell your daddy. Tell me, you cunt."

Awake now, too, Andrea lays still next to Kate as they wait to hear more of Sally's screams. When it gets really bad, sometimes they come out of the bedroom. But David gets so mad, they're afraid to go out. They only leave when their fear for their Mom outweighs their fear for themselves.

Her face pressed into his thigh, her hair pulled tight by his hand, Sally speaks muffled by his leg so close to her mouth. "Baby, I wasn't good. I was bad. I thought of bad things."

Suddenly taken by Sally's words, David

gently traces his finger around her lips. "Yeah?"

"I thought of bad things. Like how bad I wanted to suck your cock. I wanted to lick it clean."

Laughing while he continues to trace her lips with his finger, David says, "You're a nasty bitch."

"Baby, you know I am. You know I want it. Please let me love you, baby. Please."

Quietly in their room the girls listen in discomfort and with humiliation to their mother saying, "Please. Please." And then of course, there is the sound of clothes being unzipped and pried from bodies. Finally the groanings of sex. Kate holds Andrea's hand, but releases it, returns to her own bed and places a pillow over her ears. Andrea focuses on the ceiling and thinks of her favorite Dr. Suess book, "The Cat in the Hat," contemplating to herself that her Dad is very much like the cat with the big crazy hat.

On the kitchen table where Sally rests on her stomach, staring at the kitchen wall, many thoughts pass through her mind as David slams his penis inside her. *Maybe I do deserve this. Maybe this is what I want to punish myself...because I am such a fucking waste. I understand this pain. I want this pain. I am David's match. Everything he can come up with I can match. I understand how his fucking brain ticks, because I've some demons of my fucking own. He may oversize me, but pound for pound I can take him on. I can like it when he fucks me. I'm that strong to handle this all. Give to me, David. I want it. I need it. Need it. Need, need. Need.*

A slight bruise on her upper lip, Sally wears David's T-shirt. Pop Tarts toasting, Sally straightens the mess in the kitchen as Kate and Andrea enter. The girls, already dressed for school, make no eye contact with Sally. The familiar dance begins. Sally stays by the sink. Andrea sits down at the table. It's a hot, hot day, so Kate gets out the box of corn flakes and sets it on the table. She fetches two bowls with two spoons, places them on the table, grabs the milk and joins Andrea at the table. After placing the toasted Pop Tarts on each of the girls' place settings, Sally pours herself a glass of milk. For a moment Sally quietly watches over her girls, and then she withdraws into herself.

Placing the glass of milk on the table Sally moves to the phone and dials the fire station. Her back to the girls, Sally paces back and forth next to the kitchen counter. "Hey, Hi...It's Sally. Who's this? Well, how's it going? Listen I wanted to talk to Ralph...or do you know if anyone from the front office is in yet?...Sure thing." Sally focuses on a dirty glass while she silently waits; scrubbing the glass, looking out the window above the sink, rinsing the glass, placing it back in the soapy water and cleaning it again. In the distance, the school bus can be heard approaching. "Hey, Hi...How's it going? Weeelll, see that's the problem. I've had this cold that I can't seem to get over. I'm thinking if I take a day or two off...Maybe I'll have the girls pick up payroll so I can work on it at home." Setting down the clean glass, Sally strokes the water on the counter with her finger tip. "...If I'm not better, by the end of today...Yeah, I didn't know you'd be in. That's why I called the fire crew. Sure. No? Do you think...well, I'll see if I can't get in there by tomorrow. If you think of anything...No, of course. Thanks Paul. Thank you." There is silence while Sally listens to her boss. "Thank you. Thanks. See you soon." And Sally hangs up the phone, crosses to the table and takes her glass of milk. Returning to washing dishes, Sally listens while the girls rise from the table, each with their Pop Tart in hand.

Scratching his naked, tanned beer belly and running his other hand through his shaggy hair, David enters like a bear coming out of hibernation. "How's my girls? Katie? Andrea? Give the old man a kiss."

Both girls say hello and kiss their father. David growls at Andrea -- which makes her giggle and makes Kate roll her eyes.

"Where you going?"

"School, Dad," says Kate.

"In summer? Damn, you're good. Sure the

hell ain't like me. I wouldn't even go to school in the school time...the school year. But look where I am. You should get yourselves to school. Become doctors or something."

"Yeah, Dad. Bye," says Kate as she takes Andrea's hand and pulls her out of the house. Kate and Andrea wave good-bye to David.

And then there is the silence and tension of two people left in a room alone together. David looks over at Sally's back while she pours out her glass of milk, and submerges it into the soapy water. "Hi, honey," he says. Sally stops and turns around. When she smiles his heart melts...and he notices her bruise. "Oh. Oh. Baby. Hurt?" Sally nods her head and tries to retrieve the huge tears that well into her eyes. David dogfacedly approaches Sally and touches her bruise with a gentle finger. "Kiss it, make it better," purrs David. Softly he presses his lips to her bruise, and they fall into a deep embrace. "I didn't mean to hurt my baby. I was just tired...crazy tired." Looking deep into Sally's eyes, he smiles and touches her more roughly -- playfully, "Crazy tired...crazy tired...crazy tired. Kiss me again." David smiles and traces his finger along Sally's lips. She watches him study her mouth...and she kisses David. Instantly, tears that were held back spill over and down Sally's face.

David murmurs, "No, baby. Baby. No. No. We're okay."

Sally pauses and wipes away her tears. "I think. Maybe we should go into social services and talk with some people. Maybe get, you know, counseling or somethi--?"

"What the fuck is wrong with you? Who you been talking with?" rages David, instantly overcome by anger.

"Why do you do that?" asks Sally, immediately defensive and teary eyed, again.

"I figured you were smarter than that."

"Smarter? Stop it. I -- that's not --"

"Who you talking about me with?"

"Nobody. I'm not stupid."

"Nobody. Yeah, sure. Fucking nobody told

you to go to family services..."

"Yeah nobody. And why can't we go? I think we should go. It'll help."

"Do you actually give a shit about our kids, cause I'll tell you one thing we walk in that door and they'll have them in a second. I mean come on, use your little head! What you think they're gonna do with Andrea and Katie? We live like model parents, don't we, Sal? CPS'll be in here so fast your head'll spin. And don't go thinking it's all me, cause that just ain't the truth. We go, and we'll fucking lose our kids."

"No, we won't."

"You know so much. What you think's gonna happen, Sherlock?"

"Nothing. We just..."

"What you think they're gonna counsel us about? Huh? You want to go? Lose your kids...lose our babies?"

"No. Okay. Forget it. It'll be fine." Sally tries to smile. "Never mind. You're right. It was a bad idea. Okay?"

Element of Blank

David squares off, preparing to give his speech. "Sal, it's like this: we got stuff to work out. Sure. But doesn't everybody? Ain't nobody perfect. The people in those offices don't know crap. Those people, they probably ain't even married. But I'll tell you what I do know: they don't fucking know me, and they don't know you. That shit is deep, you know -- it's real. And they go and try and put us into a formula or some such shit, and take away our girls. So, yeah, we got stuff to work out." Putting his hand behind Sally's head, "Just don't go around threatening me, okay? It'll work out." David smiles and looks into Sally's eyes, "Won't it?"

"Yeah. You know I want it to work out."

"Well, don't worry so much. You know I love you. Don't you?"

Sally looks at David, the familiar curve of his lips and the roughness of his chin. "Yeah. I know you love me." She smiles resignation when he leans in and kisses her neck.

In low population areas its not uncommon for the government to practice "illegal" tests. This area, obviously low in population, constantly gets slammed by sonic booms. Stretched out in the lawn chair on desert earth, Sally nestled inside David's chest, a bold crack thuds through the crystal blue sky. The jet had passed a few seconds before. The noise shouldn't have been a surprise, but it was. It always is. It doesn't ever matter how expected it may be, you're never braced for it.

"Jesus Christ, those fuckers!" shouts David. Pushing Sally off him, he climbs out of the chair and goes inside the house. He returns with his bag which he throws on the ground. "I know they're in here somewhere. Worm set me up."

While David searches his bag Sally eyes him. And she knows the cycle is complete. *Back together at last. I thought for a second I could...what an asshole I am. Total utter ass. It'll always come to this moment, and I will always be here. Full circle. Here's looking at you, kid. Together forever. Till the fucking end, Right? I need this. I need him. I need us. I need this to breathe. Who the hell cares? What possible difference does any of this make? I need us. Need him. I do.*

"It's your lucky day, my little bean," says David as he pulls out a brown paper sack with some medicine bottles, a syringe, four baggies of white and pink pills, and a blue foil package. "Get me a beer and a spoon."

Sally rises and walks numbly into the house. Opening the refrigerator door, everything appears as though it's in a commercial. As if this life in which she takes action, isn't hers at all, but another. A gambling life in which risks and actions are taken which Sally would never take. Grabbing the bottle of beer, Sally shuts the refrigerator door. She grabs a glass from the dish rack and carefully fills it with slow running water. Watching the water overflow onto her hand, she smiles and lets it keep running. Outside David stirs. Turning off the water Sally dries her hand on her shirt and grabs a spoon from the rack of dishes, picks up the glass of water and the beer.

His belt around his arm, he takes the spoon from Sally,"God damn, I got fucking old waiting. You got lead in your ass or what?" David grabs Sally's thigh, bites it with a huge, soft mouth and laughs.

Ignoring him, Sally hands David the beer and grabs one of the baggies. "No. I just got distracted. Which one do I take?"

"You're going with me."

"Okay. Will you do me?"

"Yeah, I'll do you. Any time, baby."

Removing the belt from his arm, he pulls Sally onto the ground next to him and takes her arm. After a second she takes a long drink of water and watches while David prepares her injection, cupping his hand to protect the flame. "Now, why we doin' this?"

"You know why. Because we understand...we unify each other. This only helps us to find our divine, holy bond. We're like the water passing through you."

"'Cept I'm just gonna piss that out," says

Sally with a smile.

"That you are, baby. That you are." David plunges the needle into Sally's arm and removes the elastic band. Her body jars slightly and then becomes serene.

David prepares his arm and injection. The needle in his vein, he smiles at Sally, "Let the games begin."

Words vanish and image overwhelms. Sally's eyes dilate and expand into her brain flooded by extreme desire and intensity. *The huge blue sky...Blue...blue,..bLUE . Too blue. Hide inside. Lay on the bed together. Bed swallows me up slanting and rolling. Why does he laugh? Why do you laugh? Don't laugh. Stir me. Entice me. Games, games. Where are all the games? Yes. I want you to take my hand. No, softer. Be firm. You see me smile. Smile. Engage. Smooth chest. Want to touch. Yes. Yes. I had forgotten...yes. Lips. Red and creamy rough smooth skin and brown stubble above the hairy beard and EARS. Ears . Strange flaps of hearing. Listen to the silence. Listen. Ears. Lips. Stomach against thigh against arm. Beautiful arm. Deep into brown eye...deeper where color separates and see...black pupil shatter to pieces. Lip of mouth stretch around and swallow me whole. Vanish me up. I feel gone. Up and away to blueness.*

Waking at about four in the afternoon, Sally sees David next to her, his naked body squashed up against the comforter. Her mouth dry and her eyes parched and throbbing, she rolls over to her back and becomes aware of her own naked form. Twisting herself into the fetal position, her back to David, Sally hears the T.V. Her body collapses for a moment as she stares motionless at the bedroom wall. Kate speaks to Andrea quietly, and Sally twists her body, forcing herself to fall out of the bed. Quietly Sally searches out clothes, a T-shirt and shorts. Wanting to leave the bedroom, but terrified to face her kids, Sally finds a pack of cigarettes in David's blue jeans. Flipping his zippo Sally sucks in the smoke. Her knees folded Indian style she sinks into a corner of the bedroom. Ashing in her nearby shoe, Sally listens to the girls watching T.V. and quietly playing their secret games. Her eyes make their way to David on the bed as he stirs and slips back to sleep.

Think about dinner. What'll we eat? How about the cover-up? I should get the payroll tonight...but I'm too tired. Take the girls. They can pick it up, but not today. The bruise isn't really that bad. I don't want to talk to them right now. Pasta? Do I have any tuna? No bread. Frozen Pizza? How do I get off the floor? There's lots of time. Got to get up and move. Jesus, girls I'm sorry. How does this happen...I hate this. I'm stuck on the floor. For Christ's sake go outside to play so I can enter my goddamn house and make dinner. I'll wait. Won't I? Can't I wait, forever? That's what I get. Forever. Pizza only takes about 40 minutes. David won't be mad. He won't be awake. At least we're a family. The girls like to have him here...especially at dinner because we're all together then. Normal. A family. Jesus.

After an hour passes Sally, having smoked half the pack of cigarettes, raps her knuckles against her head. She rises and makes her way down the narrow hallway gliding her hand along the wall, making a warning noise for the girls to hear her approach. When she enters the kitchen they turn their ghost eyes and look at her. Sally glances at them, expressionless, and yanks open the freezer door. Peeling off the cardboard seal Sally goes to the oven and turns it on, returns to the pizza box, checks the suggested temperature, and adjusts the dial. Shifting through the cupboards Sally tries to find the cookie sheet.

"You girls," says Sally in a raspy, unused voice, "You girls know where the baking sheets got to?"

The girls shake their heads no.

"Well it didn't just up and walk away, did it? Fine. I guess we don't need it."

The pizza box in her hand, Sally reads the directions. She keeps losing her train of thought, and rereading the box. Taking the pizza out from inside, Sally tears the plastic wrap with her teeth. Frozen pizza in the oven -- Presto. Sally slams shut the oven door and glances around the house catching the back of her girls' heads as they watch T.V. Wanderlessly moving through the house, Sally grabs her pack of cigarettes and walks outside to the lawn chair in back.

The evening coolness is about an hour and a half away, but the steadiness of the warmth has become softer already. A black crow flies overhead chased by or maybe flying with another smaller bird, a sparrow maybe. Sally wonders how this can happen...how a smaller animal can be so protective that they can force a larger animal from their nest. That's what she believes has happened. And then there is stillness. A roaring quiet.

I've got to get this promotion. We'll be fine. I can put money in a savings account. I'll open one that David doesn't know about. The girls and I can go away. We'll go to L.A. or New York , maybe. Or maybe just Utah or something. I could get a job with the Forest Service there. With my promotion they'll want to transfer me. I'll have the asset of my training. But maybe that would be too easy for David to trace. If I could find a way for us to disappear...he'd give up eventually...maybe. Maybe he wouldn't care. If I could find him a bag of drugs big enough to last a year...he could find some pathetic crotch...he'd be distracted. We'll show him. I'm the sparrow. I can overcome him...together we'll overpower this life. We'll live on the beach and play hours in the sand and lick salt water on our lips. It'll be beautiful. The girls'll look up to me then. They'll be able to trust me, and I won't let them down anymore. We'll be fearless...free...and they'll know I got them away. I got them away.

David slams the door shut behind him. "What you thinking about?"

Sally says nothing and closes her eyes, soaking in the last of today's warmth.

"Hey, Stupid?"

"What?"

"Forget it. When we having dinner?"

"It's in the oven. About ten minutes."

"That was hot today, baby. You are so hot. I love your fucking nasty body. You like it?"

"Yeah. Sure. I'm going inside. The girls might have questions on their homework."

"Like you'd be able to answer...What's up your ass anyway? I come out here and talk all nice and you go off acting like a bitch."

Sally leans down and kisses David's mouth. "Sorry. I just shouldn't have missed work today. We need the money. I was feeling guilty."

"You don't need to ever work, okay? They don't fucking own you. Christ, the way they make you feel. I should just make you quit."

"But baby, it don't make sense. Besides they like me there. It's fine. I'm just in a mood. Maybe it's my period soon or something."

"May fucking be. Well, help the little kiddies with their summer school homework...maybe you can help them color inside the lines!" David laughs.

With a smile Sally says, "May fucking be." She turns and leaves David alone in the desert, his laughter cut short.

Sally sets the table for four, something which delights her...in spite of herself. In the living room the girls watch Knight Rider, their favorite show. They're fighting about whether it's better to have Michael Knight for a boyfriend, or just have the car...because without Kit, Michael's just a regular guy. Andrea thinks it's better to have Michael for a boyfriend because Kit, the car, comes with him; Kate believes Kit could be her friend, why not cut out the boyfriend and have the car for yourself?

Andrea retorts Kate's position by saying, "But he comes with Kit. You can't separate them. Kit is Michael's car."

"Alright, enough. Dinner's ready in ten minutes. I want you to get cleaned up."

Sullenly the girls stop their fighting and look at Sally.

"So you're back to being a mom again?" says Kate.

Without thinking, Sally rushes over to Kate and slaps her mouth. Dead in her tracks, Sally looks at Kate's shocked expression. "I'm sorry, Katie. Jesus...fucking Christ. I'm sorry."

"I know. Forget..." Kate's eyes well with tears as she backs away from Sally. "Come on," says Kate as she pulls Andrea along with her to the bathroom.

Sally watches them leave, her face pale and her gut twisted. Inside the oven, a quarter of the pizza drops through the metal rack onto the broiler. The cheese starts to burn, causing the house to smoke up. With hot pads Sally removes the rest of the pizza onto three plates she fans together. She tosses the pizza on the counter and slices it.

In the bathroom, Andrea (clean faced) watches Kate wash her hands and face. Looking in the mirror Kate examines her cheek, expecting a mark and finding nothing.

"Does it hurt?"

"Kinda. I hate her sometimes, Andrea."

"Me, too."

"No you don't. You're just saying that."

Andrea watches Kate's reflection staring at her in the mirror. "I think I hate him," says Andrea carefully.

"Yeah. I guess. Me, too. I don't know."

"I hate him."

"Well, if we had Kit we could run over him...but Michael Knight wouldn't let us do that. So it's better to have the car without the guy." Andrea laughs, and after bumping Andrea with her hip, Kate smiles a giggle.

Dinner's served.   Pizza and an iceberg lettuce salad with ranch dressing. David arrives late. Everyone seated at the table...waiting; each plate already portioned up: one piece for each of the girls, one for Sally and the rest for David. The house stinks with smokiness; their eyes burn a little.

"Jesus Christ, Sally.   Got to charcoal everything? Can we open a door or something? Fucking smoke. Thanks for waiting for me." Sally rises to open up the doors, David takes a seat and starts eating.

Sally returns and there is silence at the table. Only the sound of smacking lips and forks digging into salad. Glancing up from her plate Sally finds Kate glaring at her. Weakly Sally exchanges the glance, but Kate won't let her eyes off of Sally. Sensing a disruption David stops eating and sees the stare off. He starts to laugh.

"Girls, girls. Be friends. What could be so bad?"

"Ask Mom. She's the one who slapped me."

"Well, I'm sure she had good reason the way you're talking back to me right now. You're too much alike. That's your problem. I don't feel like getting into this. Just shut up and eat your dinner."

Kate drops her gaze and stares at her plate. After a moment of pause David returns to eating...followed by everyone else.

His dinner complete, David sighs. Sally raises up from the table and collects the plates.

When she passes by her, Sally strokes the side of Kate's face. Kate flinches, but Sally rests her hand on Kate's shoulder for a long second. Kate stands up and follows Sally to the sink. Pushing herself near her mother, Kate says, "I know you didn't mean it." Sally hugs Kate warmly.

"That's the way, girls. That's the way," says David as he tickles Andrea, who giggles gleefully at his attention.

"Hi, Sally. Wanta help?" says Julie, paint bucket in hand, wearing paint-splattered Nomex pants. "We're painting today. Those bozos think that I'm going to do a good job. I think we're gonna have a paint party."

"Hey, hi." Sally smokes a cigarette next to the coke machine. "Women do make the best edgers. Got better control." Holding a pretend brush Sally mimics gently dabbing the brush on the wall. "My husband always has me edge. We're more detail."

"Guess I don't have that gene working for

me. I'm more paint on the floor." Both women laugh. "Well...better get on it."

"What you painting?"

"The information box. Oh yeah, it's a slow season alright. We don't even have weeds to pull. Gotta wait for them to grow. See you."

Sally nods. "See you." Stepping on her cigarette butt, Sally enters the back door of the front office. She walks over to her supervisor's open door, pokes her head in and knocks. "I think I'll head home and be back early in the A.M. See you, Paul."

"You going to be in tomorrow?"

"Yeah -- the whole day. I'll give you a call if something comes up. But I'm sure I'll be in. Bye."

It's eleven o'clock in the morning and Sally promised to make David lunch. She rushes to the bank to cash her check. Sally wants to open an account of her own...the secret account. *What if he found out? I can't...'cause he'll find out. How can I explain a whole other account? He'll just find out about it and take the money somehow. I shouldn't. But*

*maybe...Maybe I can talk to someone about keeping it
confidential. Like it's a surprise for my kids. Like it's an
education fund...but they'd let David know about that...*
A handful of people on their lunch break wait
patiently for their turn, and barely turn their heads
as Sally pries open the glass doors and steps into
the coolness of the bank. The slow milling pace
sucks Sally into the line, and while her eyes dart at
the clock frantically, the lunch hour begins to
approach. Finally at 11:25 it's her turn at the
window. Jean waves her over.

"How we doing today, Sally?"

"Fine. Running errands...running behind."

"Ain't that just the way it is."

"Yeah."

"So do you want any cash back?"

"Yeah...I want it all back."

"You going outta town?" asks Jean as she
counts back the money. "Twenties okay?"

"Can I get two hundred of it in hundred
dollar bills?"

"Sure."

"Six hundred and twenty dollars...and thirty eight cents."

"Thanks."

"Now you have a good time."

Sally nods and inside she feels a spark of excitement. It could be that easy, she smiles to herself.

Sally parks on Main Street just outside the Mexican restaurant. The tourists have filled it up -- the line stretches to the door. After shifting her weight back and forth, nervously adjusting her underwear through her pants, Sally finally orders two tacos to go and a side of rice and beans. The time is 11:50. The volunteer fire alarm/noon bell rings as Sally slides into her Jeep, carefully balancing the styrofoam box on the passenger seat, she takes her two hundred dollar bills and shoves them up inside the lining of the seat. Jamming on the gas Sally flips a U-turn and makes her way out of town into her outskirt neighborhood. The neighbor from two houses down, Jesse, rides his horse. He raises his hand to Sally, and she raises hers to him. The Jeep roars onto the driveway, pulling to an abrupt stop.

David comes to the door. "Where the fuck were you?!"

Jesse walks by on the horse, ignoring the fight. Clump, Ka-clomp. Clump, Ka-clomp. Clump, Ka-clomp, with his eyes straight ahead.

Shouting at Sally, because she's turned her back to him, David bellows, "Hello, fat ass. How you going to make me lunch when you know I like to eat before noon?"

Sally stands still, watching Jesse ride past. Turning to David she says under her breath, "Here, you fat pig. Your lunch is ready." Passing him in the doorway, Sally hands David the styrofoam box, which he allows to drop to the ground.

Once inside the house David pushes Sally hard so that she bumps into the wall. "What did you call me?"

"Nothing."

"Didn't sound like it."

"But it looks like it."

"What the fuck's that supposed to mean? What...am I nothing? Is that what you're saying?"

"Did I say that? I don't think I said that."

"What do you think you are?"

"I think you should go...I don't want you here with the girls...they...we don't want you...'

"What the fuck you saying?"

"I don't know."

"Sounds like you fucking know. Who you been talking to? I'll kick their mother-fucking ass."

"What do I need? I got a brain, David. I can figure shit out. I don't need to talk to someone to know you treat me bad."

"I treat you bad? I treat you bad?" David is silent as the rage quickly fills him. "You, fucking bitch, don't have an idea how bad, bad is. I am so good to you. You don't even see it. Always wanting fucking something more."

Sally retreats. *It's coming...it'll be bad...there's no way out of it...I hope, pray he won't bash my head in...don't let that happen, God. I know I fucked up. It's my fault. Just let me live. I'll give him the money from my truck. I'll be good. I won't talk back if you let me live so that my girls don't find me dead on the kitchen floor. Please.*

Like an animal David feels Sally retreat. He picks up the phone book and throws it at her. She jumps back. And he laughs. "Where's all your toughness gone to? Big plans falling through? You want to fight so bad, let's fucking fight!" David pushes the kitchen chair at Sally. She avoids it, and he pushes it at her more violently. The chair slams against Sally's hip. Sally folds in pain. Walking right up to her, David looks at Sally for a while. Then he lunges and takes her by the hair. He throws her against the kitchen counter, causing Sally to strike her left eye against the cupboard handle. She sinks down in a heap to the floor.

"I don't want to fight, David."

"What's that?"

"I don't want to fight."

"Changing your story, now? Because you sure as fuck wanted to fight before."

"I was wrong."

"You were wrong? How do you think you made me feel? Like some fucking horror who you don't want to touch your kids. My kids." David kicks Sally twice in the side. She screams in pain and crawls over to the corner next to the hallway...close to the door. Picking Sally up by her arm, his grip constricted around her petite limb, he punches her once, twice, three times, connecting with the side of her head, her eyes, her mouth, her cheek and her ear.

"Never underestimate me. Ever." David shoves Sally onto the ground, goes to the bedroom and throws some laundry into his bag. He returns to find Sally huddled in the corner, her hands cupped over the shrill ringing in her ear. "You got any money. I'm gone for a while."

Sally nods and thinly she says, "In my purse. It's most of the pay check. I need it for rent."

"What the fuck were you trying to pull? You gonna just trip away...like I wouldn't notice?

Like I wouldn't find you? Huh?" David pockets two hundred and fifty dollars.

"No."

David looks at Sally and laughs. "You're fucking pathetic. Don't try things you can't accomplish. You don't have what it takes to make it on your own, Sal. That's why you got me. I'll be back later." Picking up his bag, David leaves.

In the corner, blood on her lips and eye and red blotches of impact covering most of her face, arms, and stomach, Sally waits. The Harley fires up and backs away. Throbbing in pain, Sally begins to sob. A mournful cry aches from her body as she slides down flat onto the cool linoleum floor. Unrestrained, Sally weeps.

Clean, wearing a nightgown, with her hair still wet, Sally lays stretched out on the couch watching "Oprah." The school bus shuttles by, coming to a halt at the end of the street and its doors open. With a badly bruised cheek, fat lip and her eye blackened and swollen shut, Sally lays still, waiting. The front door opens and the girls enter. Tossing their packs next to the door they enter with smiles on their faces, ready to watch T.V.

"Mom?" asks Kate, her smile vanished.

"It's okay, honey," says Sally, her fat lip making her words form thick, and her mouth move oddly.

The girls come and stand next to Sally. Leaning against the couch, Kate pushes up against Sally's hand and Andrea carefully places herself at the end of the couch next to Sally's feet. Both the girls start to cry.

"Now what good is that going to do? Come here, Katie. Spoon with me and we'll watch Oprah."

Cautiously Kate sits on the couch with her small back to Sally. Laying on her side, she curls into Sally's body. Wincing at the pressure to her bruises Sally says,"There, that's better. I'm sorry."

"Mom?"

"Yeah?"

"Is he gone?"

"Yeah. For a while."

"What are we gonna do?"

"Kate, don't ask me that. I don't know. He just lost his temper. And he's cooling off now. We'll be just fine. Bruises heal, right?"

"Right."

"Well, that's all these are. And I do promise...it won't be like this forever. Maybe he'll change or maybe something else, but it won't be like this forever. Okay?"

Kate and Andrea watch the T.V. silently.

around the corner

This time of year sunrise happens just after five in the morning. The rays burn and burn to crack over the granite mountains and flood their light onto the sleeping valley below. Scampering back into the sage brush outside of the town, the silhouette of the coyotes and raccoons can be seen every morning. A local Indian woman once explained that looking directly at a coyote is bad luck. Probably theories like that would vary from tribe to tribe. This morning, however, the coyote brought luck. The best kind -- hope.

Sally, bruised and bundled in a blanket, walks over the cold morning ground to the lawn chair to enjoy the birth of a new day. Her chair squeaking with coldness, Sally tries to hold still. She wants this moment to be special...near religious if possible. Meditating on her new hope, Sally doesn't hear the skittish and dainty steps of the coyote walking behind her. It isn't until she is within six inches of Sally that they both become aware of each other. In mutual respect and terror, they are still. Cracking mildly over the mountains (lighting the sky -- not yet the valley), the sun sends golden rays warming the sad, old mountains in the east, turning them a pinky orange. In the darkness the coyote stays beside Sally long enough for the morning light to brighten and reveal the texture of its coat and the sharpness of its long nose. And as quietly as it came, the coyote pads away into the sage brush. But for Sally it's significant because she feels touched by magic. She feels certain the bad is in the past and the good has arrived at last...and she must invite it into her life.

"Hello? Hey...I need to talk to Ralph. It's Sally. Thanks." Sally stands in the kitchen. Kate and Andrea have already gone to catch the bus. "Ralph, can you talk? This'll take a second." Starting to shake, Sally finds her way to a chair. "Thanks. So I need to ask you a favor. My problem is that I'm a little...a...I got beat up...No, of course not...It was David. He just lost his temper. But I promise, and I mean it this time, to not put up with this any more. But I need your help. I've got a huge black eye...I can't go to work, but I need your advice...between you and me. Please?" Sally listens and shakes her head, wanting to speak, but holding quiet. "But I don't think Paul would understand this. Not that you do, Ralph...but you're not judgmental. I'm afraid. I know I can't afford to miss any more work -- but I've never messed up payroll and...Okay. You're right. I guess I'll have to come down there. Thanks. Bye."

Sally hangs up the phone and goes to her bedroom mirror. *Sunglasses? What a cliche of the beaten woman. Is that what I've become?* Without thinking anymore, Sally carefully puts on her pants and a long-sleeved cotton shirt to cover her bruises, and slips into sandals. She puts make-up over her puffy, full lips and powder over her eye, but it doesn't help. Putting on her sunglasses she takes one last look. *You are the cliche. And you're not fooling anybody. Who are you anyway?* Grabbing her keys she collects her courage and goes outside.

Sally parks along Main Street -- away from the compound and the fire crew. She doesn't want to even be here...the last thing she wants is for everyone to see her in this undone state. Entering through the front desk (the information desk) no one really notices her. Quickly moving through the office she sees "Yosemite Sam" approach her. Tucking her head down, she makes a quick left and then a right into the bathroom. With shallow, panicked breaths, she locks herself inside the stall. *I could just go. No one deserves this of me. I won't be humiliated. Paul will only look at me with those strange foreign eyes of surprise and say to himself, "I understand what you are all about now." But I 'm not. I'm not an abused woman. This was a fight...it got out of control. I don't need to do this. I could quit. But I don't want to. I love this job. These are my people. I've got to, but Lord do I have to do this?*

Calming herself, she unlocks the door and walks to Paul's office. Fortunately, he's there and no one else is. She enters and closes the door behind her. Talking on the phone, Paul glances up at Sally, smiles and raises his hand. She takes a seat. After a few minutes, Paul hangs up the phone. He notices something wrong with Sally's face, but tries not to let on.

"What can I do you for?"

"Paul...this is so hard. I...it's fine...for you to notice...it's why I'm here. To tell you."

"What are you talking about?"asks Paul,

sincerely.

"I'm sorry. Christ, I'm nervous. My husband was upset with...well, we had a fight. He lost his temper...and I'm so sorry to do this but I need some time off...more time off. I can't come to work like this. I'm sure that Ralph'll bring me any of the paperwork I need...it's just I'm not fit to be at work..."

"Well, okay. I understand. You can't work like this. Of course, I understand. Work things out with Ralph and I'll give you the time off. You still got sick leave?"

"A bit. Listen, this won't be a problem. Ralph'll help."

"Well, I'll make sure you get the sick leave, okay?"

"Thanks, Paul. Thank you. I was so scared that you wouldn't understand -- never mind. Thank you."

"If you need anything: ask. Okay?"

"This won't happen again. My job is too important to me...I hate missing work. It won't happen again."

"Well, I hope so. Not for the job or our sake, Sally...but for yours."

Taking pause Sally looks into Paul's kind, uncomfortable eyes. She hugs Paul and then props open the door again. "Thank you." From behind her sunglasses, Sally walks out of the office her head high, and scans the desks and personnel. Waving once at Viki, she walks back through the hallway, passes through the information booth, and makes her way back to her Jeep. A tremendous weight lifted, she feels the rebuilding has begun. *The cat is out of the bag and I'm not going to be fired. We're going to be okay. Thank you, God! Thank you.*

When they get home from school Sally drives the girls into town and lets them shop for their own dinner, which she cooks for them at home. They eat fish sticks and french fries with twinkies for dessert...a whole box. As the sun finally sets Sally digs out three melted, dusty candles from inside the kitchen utility drawer and places them in three separate bowls.

"Go put on dresses for dancing, girls. We're going to have a party, tonight. Today is a special day. This day is the day of the coyote. And we're going to celebrate it."

Although it seems a bit odd to them, the girls are excited to get dressed up. So they run to their room. The living room is full of flickering candle light when Kate returns wearing her J.C. Penny's dress, white with blue flowers on the neck and a few minutes later Andrea comes dressed in her sheer yellow nightgown, her baby fat and flowery underpants visible underneath.

"My goodness, you two are so beautiful," says Sally. And she means it. The girls giggle. "Now all we need is music...and if I may, I shall select the music. I will be the disc jockey tonight." Sally speaks in a goofy voice and the girls laugh, because they don't know this side of their mother.

The eject button snaps in and the cassette deck opens. Looking at the tape, Sally places it inside and fast forwards. Although this night is for the girls...this song is for her. It is the connection with a former Sally...when she was a teenager and free and full of expectation. A frown forms on her face as she considers the Sally of today. When she presses play it's still the wrong song, but it's approaching the end. The girls make disco moves and dance with each other. Sally watches and smiles, and laughs at their clowning. Then her song comes on, the beautiful BeeGees singing "How Deep Is Your Love?" Sally closes her eyes and starts to move to the music, while Kate and Andrea watch this beautiful stranger in their mother's skin.

When I see your eyes in morning sun
I feel you touch me in the pouring rain...
And you come to me on a summer breeze
keep me warm in your love...
And it's me you need to show
How deep is your love?...
I really need to learn.
Because we're living in world of fools

breaking us down

when they all should let us be.

we belong to you and me.

How deep is your love? How deep is your love?

How deep is your love?

I really need to learn...

we belong to you and me.

And then the next groovin' tune comes on, "Night Fever." And the girls break into a dance. Free, uninhibited, open.   The strange walls of parent/child disappear and magic drips off the ceiling, exploding beyond silly music, fancy dresses, and Sally's bruises. The girls see their mother dance, and everyone knows even as the moment plays on that they will treasure the weirdness of this evening, forever. It is their own.

Sally has always regarded her existence as a fast paced machine, beyond her control. Given that Sally's life speeds by twisting at a roller coaster pace, times of happiness and fast-moving heights are particularly terrifying, because of the knowledge that just beyond a bend, just to the left of an exciting, fun loop, may rest a sharp cliff. So the height serves as added terror from which one will plummet -- crashing through an unknown, dark place until finally bottoming out and slowing down and leaving the happiness behind. For Sally the frustration rests always in her greedy want for the happiness to continue, and the seasoned thoughts in the back of her mind that keep screaming: *Don't go down that road, look at the green light twice before driving, don't eat chocolate cake, don't forget to kiss the girls...because you know the cliff is right behind the missing or the doing of certain actions.* With every moment celebrated Sally keeps her eye on the door, waiting for the crash to begin. But it doesn't. For three days, then a week, then three weeks, and finally a month, Sally keeps a sideways eye on the door, but it stays shut.

In a strange way Sally begins to miss David. Not so much him, but the knowledge that he was a part of her life. She isn't sure if he'll ever come back. He'll probably come back...David would never just let her be, he doesn't work like that. But something in the length of his separation makes her confused...as if a factor on which her life has been almost solely based, is now absent. Sally mourns the loss of her man late at night as she crawls into bed. Her bruises newly healed, she doesn't want David back, but she does long to understand what had been. So she lives with that understanding, or rather that lack of understanding, and with an acceptance of her new life. Keeping her habit of celebration with her eye on the door, Sally becomes less and less worried that her door will open.

Restaurants in town are pretty limited. Coffee shops, fast food (Frosty's North and South), and a couple nicer places where for some reason the Locals don't eat (too expensive and full of Europeans). As far as coffee shops go, there's about three that change hands and names on a regular basis. And then there's BamBam's Bonanza: a staple in this community for as long as anyone can remember. Location of every Lion's Club event, place of infinite graduation and prom night dinners, the site of countless P.T.A. meetings...in fact it's the only place in town that "caters" events in its special board room. The well washed windows and the newly painted exterior give a false impression of the food inside. But never mind that...all the locals know the food's often barely fit to eat, they only come because it's the place. Been there forever, been coming there forever.

Sally's Jeep pulls into a parallel parking space in front of BamBam's right in the center of town. Racing each other to the front door Kate and Andrea fly out of the Jeep and crash inside the coffee shop. Although it's early evening, about five thirty, the red booths are already filling up with old, broken-down cowboys, teenage girls, town bachelors, and curious tourists. Kate and Andrea fall silent as they enter and stand next to the cashier's stand while waiting for Sally to catch up with them.

This is the first night that Sally's bruises are healed enough to be seen in public. Pleased to be free from her exile, Sally follows the girls to a booth, and slides onto the thick, well-worn, red vinyl. Within a few minutes, Barbie, the town's main and only true career waitress, walks up to them and slaps down an ammonia-soaked rag on the table.

"Yeah? What'd ya want?" she barks. Barbie knows everyone by name, but doesn't bother with the formalities. For her, it's enough that she's spent the last twenty-nine years of her life serving these people. Forget questions and answers and name dropping to show she pays attention. She knows, of course she knows...she just doesn't care.

"Can we have menus, please?" asks Sally.

In a huff Barbie spins around in her orthopedic shoes and walks to the cashier island grabbing three puffy, red, vinyl-wrapped menus. Andrea studies Barbie's hair, which despite its thinness is piled and wrapped and sprayed into a remarkable beehive. Returning with the menus, Barbie grabs her gray rag and sweeps it across the table, causing Sally and the girls to lean back and hold up their arms. Delighted to be so close to her hair, Andrea wrenches her neck to get a closer look. Apparently unaware, Barbie straightens up, sets the menus down and departs.

"That's rude," says Kate slapping Andrea from across the table with her menu.

"What?"

"Staring."

"Was not."

"Were, too."

"Girls, shhh!"

"But mom, she was staring at the waitress' hair," whispers Kate.

Wanting desperately not to, Sally is unable to avoid laughing when she goes to question Andrea about her behavior. Further delighted, Andrea joins into the laughter.

"Mom, that's not fair. You never laugh

when I do things like that."

"Katie," says Sally from behind stifled laughter, "Honey, you're right. Andrea, honey, you shouldn't look at...the waitressss..."Sally starts to laugh again. And this time Kate joins in, too. The three girls giggle and laugh and start to relax, only to begin again.

In a few minutes Barbie returns and again asks, "So...What'd ya want?"

Focusing with all her energy on the menu, Sally says, "May I have...," and her face twists into a smile with a laugh on her lips, "Let's see, how about a salad with ranch dressing. And a Diet Coke." Proudly Sally closes her menu and stares at Kate with an expression of bet-you-can't-keep-from-laughing, with a hint of a parental don't-you-dare-laugh. Deadpan, Kate orders a grilled cheese sandwich with french fries, and closes her menu with a glance of superiority to Sally. Finally, it's Andrea's turn and of course, beyond her control, Andrea stares at Barbie's hair.

With dreamy eyes, Andrea places her order.

"May I have french fries and a coke and a *cheese booger*?"

"You wouldn't mean a cheeseburger would you there, sugar?" asks Barbie.

Kate breaks into a loud, warm, laugh and then Sally joins in, too. Even Barbie cracks a smile. Her face blushing red, Andrea giggles, too, somehow aware she is the cause of the laughter.

Sally places her hand on top of Andrea's head and all three laugh with easiness and joy. "What a bunch of nuts!" says Sally.

With bruises behind her, Sally can finally return to work. And she can't wait. The two and a half weeks stuck at home have been long and often dull, with nothing to do but evaluate her life and try to make things happen by thinking about them. Monday morning her Jeep drives onto the Forest Service parking lot.

"Hey, you! Where the hell ya been?! We missed you," says Stan walking out of the fire office as Sally hops out of her Jeep.

"Needed a little time off. You been able to cope without me?"

"Hell no. 'Course not."

"Thought so,"says Sally with a smile. "You boys haven't even been busy. I've looked at your time cards."

"Don't be saying 'boys.' Julie or Tina might hear...then you'll hear a God-damn ruckus. That's all we need...one more reason to be at each other."

"You all work too hard. Smile now. You're getting to be as fragile as Viki. Speaking of which, how's it been with her these past couple of weeks?"

"Fragile? I wouldn't quite put it like that. Not really put in nice words like that. It's been. Guess that's all I can say. We been razzing Jerry about her. Saying she's got the hots for him. That gets him so mad all he can do when she comes around is stare at his feet and suck on his lips behind them glasses of his. He gets spitting mad. Walks out of the office. Actually we been having a grand time of it."

Sally laughs as Stan recounts the story to

her, "You haven't made her feel bad though? Have you?"

"Hell, no. She doesn't even know half of what goes on in the universe...but I guess I don't need to be telling you about her."

"No...guess you don't. Good seeing ya, Stan. Say 'hi' to the boys...everybody. Where are they?"

"Doing P.T.'s. I hurt my knee. Never was much of a runner, but Ralph's a long legged horse...always wants to run 'em. I said 'Fine. Only I'm not coming with.' Ralph just nodded. So they're out running."

"Great. Tell Ralph to come and see me."

"You two married or what?"

"Pretty much." Sally walks to the front office as Stan walks to the T.V. room.

Viki stares at Sally. She's been asking for an explanation all day, and hasn't gotten word one. There was even a secret meeting with Ralph, and she was pretty sure Sally was crying, but she couldn't tell for sure, because the door was closed. Finally Sally sits at her desk, with the office empty -- the work day over. There is only the sound of people outside on the compound settling down for the day, laughing in the barracks.

"It's just been hard without you here," says Viki finally in her quietest voice. "And I thought you were my friend. I thought you'd tell me anything."

Sally keeps her eyes on her purse, "Lets go outside and talk then. I got to smoke." Without speaking anymore, Viki follows Sally to the coke machine outside. Sally is deep in thought as she sucks in the burning embers.

"So? Why? You sick? What's going on?"

"Am I sick? What makes you...I guess I can understand. No. I am not sick. A lunatic, sick in the head, but not sick of the body." Sally laughs at her joke and drags again, while Viki's eyes question her. "Fine. You and me are friends. Nobody knows about this except for Ralph and Paul. I'm trusting you here."

Viki's eyes light up with this information, and her posture settles in for a good piece of gossip, "Okay."

"I couldn't come in because I looked like road kill."

"What?"

Sally laughs. "I looked like road kill. Like someone'd taken a dirt bike and driven all over me. 'Cept it wasn't." Sally turns and looks at Viki and breaks into another laugh. "Oh, honey. I don't mean to confuse you. It isn't that complex...My husband beat me up."

"Oh, my gosh. I...I don't know...I'm so sorry,"says Viki.

"It's in the past. 'Sides you didn't have a thing to do with it...I don't think," winks Sally.

Uncomfortable, Viki laughs and Sally joins.

"So there you go. Now you know everything about me."

Viki starts to cry.

"What you doing that for?" asks Sally.

The sobs continue for a while. "I can't

imagine. Why would he hurt you? You're so nice. And pretty."

"I don't know."

A silence falls with Sally's words and both women think -- Viki thinks between small heaving outbursts of emotion, and Sally thinks quietly, disengaged from everything except Viki's last question.

"I better pick up the girls," announces Sally finally.

"Wait. Sally. You should know I ain't gonna say shit to anyone about you. Your secret is safe with me. I am your friend. If you ever need someone to talk to...come to me."

"Thank you, Viki. That means a lot. A lot."

"Good." And Viki thrusts her large arms around Sally, but this time Sally sinks into her arms and smiles. Their awkward embrace lasts a while and when they separate there is a long silence.

"I'm going to pick up the girls," says Sally as she walks toward her car.

"Bye," says Viki holding up her hand

weakly as Sally climbs into the driver's seat.

Splashing in the water and laughing, the girls fling pieces of lake scum at each other. Bam! Kate nails Andrea right in the face, and Andrea stops in mid-laugh with a mournful, tearful scream. Sally had seen the game coming to this for the last fifteen minutes. Standing up on her towel, Sally dashes madly for the water making siren noises. Crashing through the water Sally makes her way to the girls. Her hand cupped, she slaps water at Andrea and Kate. Instead of making Andrea stop crying, Sally's actions intensify the tears. Siren noises still ringing from her mouth, Sally attempts to tickle Andrea, but Andrea turns her child's back and wades her way to the shore, leaving Kate and Sally quiet in the water.

"You are such a butthead," says Sally dripping wet, standing next to the beach towel. "Why are you crying? It was only water."

"'Cause you were ganging up on me."

"Andrea! How was I ganging up on you when I was splashing both of you?"

Silent with her tears, Andrea shrugs her shoulders.

"Okay. Move over, you little brat. I need to work on my tan, if all you want to do is sulk and whine."

Squatting down, Sally pushes Andrea over and stretches out beside her. The day is very overcast; the desert sun only a fiery ball filtered by a thick layer of gray atmosphere. The air is hot and humid. After a few moments lying next to each other the sky booms with thunder. In a few minutes the thunder rumbles again, and then magnificent lightning streaks through the air clashing into the high mountains. The powerful, gray clouds thicken in a matter of minutes. And the warm air around the lake drops temperature by fifteen degrees. Suddenly there is the smell of desert rain, followed just as suddenly by heavy and huge drops of rain beginning slowly and then flooding down fiercely. Under the cottonwood trees that surround the lake, Sally and the girls take shelter and watch the raindrops hit the lake -- the water covered with frantic, splashing ripples.

As suddenly and completely as it had begun, the rain stops, leaving behind only the distinct smell of summer rain and warm, wet asphalt. Shaking the wet towel free of muddy sand, Sally puts on her shorts and sandals. Filing to the top of the hill, the girls make their way to the parking area. Everyone climbs into the Jeep.

As Sally drives she experiences a knowledge that he will be home. By examining her posture, Sally knows Kate senses it, too. Making her way through town Sally drives very slowly, with fear and dread. But as she drives up their road, she floors the gas, excited to discover if indeed David has returned. Silently all three are aware that he will be home, and all three crane their necks in search of his Harley.

It is there, parked in its regular spot. And as the Jeep pulls up the driveway the door flies open. David stands with wild hair and a huge grin on his face, "How the hell are my ladies!?!"

Leaping out of the Jeep, Andrea runs over to David. Glancing at Sally's tense smile, Kate gets out of her seat and walks over to David, who grabs her in a huge, bear hug. David looks over at Sally sitting in the Jeep...inspecting her. Between them there is a brief stare-off. Breaking the connection, Sally fiddles with her keys in the ignition and David follows the girls into the house.

Focusing on the dirty dishes in the sink, Sally avoids eye contact with David. Still she can hear him playing with Kate and Andrea in the living room. Inside her, his presence evokes the familiar stirrings of anger and happiness. Out of the corner of her eye she can see Andrea gleefully dangling from his outstretched arm. Wanting to yell and smile all at once she lets the warm dishwater soak on her skin. Taking a sponge, she traces the edge of a green plastic glass. Then she feels his heat, then his breath on the back of her neck. Not melting into him, she continues washing the dishes in the sink, and he backs away. She can feel his eyes sizing her up.

"You sure look good, Sal. Then again, you always do. I don't want you getting a big head, but you are one foxy lady."

Sally says nothing, continues washing, and after a few seconds have passed, his eyes are still on her, she flashes him a disapproving glance of irritation.

"So it's like that," says David. "That's cool. That's cool. It's my bad. I know better than to give a lady attention she don't want. That right, girls? Man aught to know when to keep his fat trap shut, right?" He looks at Kate and Andrea who are quiet, watching the exchange between their parents. "Now don't you two start in, too. You're all damn happy to see me, and I'm happy to see my ladies. Just let it be, Sal. Girls, your mom and me have got some talking to do. Isn't she beautiful though, girls?"

Andrea nods her head, while Kate studies

David's smiling face.

There is a silence while David studies Sally, making his plan of attacks. "Can't you give an old lover a hug, at least? I promise it's all I want. Christ, I been driving on that fucking bike, thinking about how it'd smell to have your skin up in my face, and your soft, lady body up against me. Come on, Sally...Honey. Give an old lover a hug."

Sally stops washing dishes, rubbing her wet hands on her pants while she watches the desert through the kitchen window. "David, you don't know what you're asking."

"Sure I do, Sally," says David, finally catching his bearings and taking command. "I want to hold the most beautiful woman I ever seen."

"Wow. Ya sure can lay on a pile of shit thick..." says Sally with her back still turned to him.

"Say what you want about me, but that ain't bullshit. That's the God's honest truth, honey. Believe me or not, I guess...but it's true. I never seen anyone prettier than you. You're like sunshine or something."

Sally laughs. "Sunshine? Wow." And now she has a smile on her face, and David can see it, even though her back is to him. He walks up to her and taps her shoulder, and she half makes a move to turn around. Placing a warm hand on her shoulder blade, David moves around and slides between Sally and the counter and pulls her up against him. Keeping herself cold and stiff in the embrace, the pressure of his hand between her shoulder blades mellows and entices her to him. *How can this be...this cannot, will not be. No. I have had enough. He hasn't changed...has he? It's the same shit. Say no. For God's sake...say no. Pull away. Pull away. PULL AWAY!*

"No," says Sally as she steps back from David. "This is as much your home as mine...so you're welcome to stay. But we aren't doing this, David. You can sleep on the couch. Or I can. But I'm not doing this. Okay?"

David looks at her with soft eyes...surprisingly soft. "I understand, Sally. I'm so sorry. Man's gotta lay in the bed he made...so to speak."

Sally laughs. "Yeah. He does."

They look at each other silently.

"Thank you for understanding. Thank you," says Sally as she returns to cleaning the dishes.

With a grin on his face, David knocks on the bedroom door. "What's a guy gotta do to get a drink around here...with a pretty lady...who he respects and doesn't want to do anything with except enjoy and joke with?"

Sally glances up and laughs through her nose. "Ask her, I guess."

"My lovely lady...please allow me to escort your queenship to the bar of your choice. Hell, I'll drive you to Reno, if you want."

"I don't think that'll be necessary. I'm a little tired, to tell you the truth."

"Now that's a bullshit story if ever I did hear one. You and me are going out on the town.

You're too much woman to be kept stuck behind these four walls." Looking at Sally sincerely he adds, "And no funny stuff. Just you and me...respectful and all that shit." Holding up his hand with charming eyebrows, "Honest injun!"

Sally laughs, again. "Christ, I mean it. You are such an ass. Alright, I'll go, but you aren't getting laid tonight. Least not by me."

Suddenly ready to pounce, David looks away down the hallway and mutters, "Enough. Fucking enough already." After a pause he turns and looks at Sally. "The point's been made. I ain't fucking you or anyone else. Jesus Christ. Let me be nice to you at least, for crying out loud."

Hearing the familiar anger seeping into his voice Sally cringes. But instead of refusing to go out with him, she decides it'll be better to not provoke him further. She takes out a clean pair of jeans from the drawer, finds her black cowboy shirt and sets them on the bed. David enters the room when she takes off her shirt. She turns her back to him, and he watches as her clothes slide over her skin.

While she sits on the edge of the bed putting on her black cowboy boots, David leans against the bedroom wall and stares at her without a smile. "You're about the fucking most beautiful thing I ever seen. Honest to God."

"David--"

"I know. I'm sorry. It just had to be said." David takes off his shirt and stands at the closet looking for something to wear. Sally is careful not to look at his body, afraid of her response to it.

Walking into the bar, with its worn and familiar tables, Sally takes a seat and David makes his way to order drinks. The faces of her girls, watching T.V. as she and David left, haunt her mind. *What are they supposed to think? What do I think? What am I thinking? But then again what is the harm in a little company? David does know how to have a good time. That much is true. My girls would be glad...if we could be friends. And who knows...maybe we could finally work things out...after we'd been friends for a long time. Maybe in a year, or so. Sure...it's okay. He hasn't changed -- yet. In time, maybe, he might. He does love me. Still does. Just have a good time.*

"You didn't used to be such a thinker, Sally," says David, placing a couple beers and shots of tequila on the table.

"Didn't, did I. Well, I got old."

"I don't think so. I think you're the sexiest woman here."

Sally laughs and David extends his hand out to her. She looks at him with surprise...never in their entire relationship has he ever asked her to dance. They've hardly ever danced together...and then only after she begs him all night long.

"You shitting me?"

"It look like I'm trying to shit you?"

Sally's face breaks into a huge smile, and she grabs his hand. Holding her hand firmly and warmly he guides her to the dance floor, stops, looks at her straight on, and doesn't move. Sally blushes and stares down at the floor.

"Stop that, you big horse's ass."

"How'd you get to be so wonderful?"

"Shut up and dance with me," says Sally with her eyes narrowing.

Moving into his arms, Sally's swallowed into David's body. Very close to her ear David's lips whisper, "Let the games begin."

Laughing, Sally steps back and shoves David in the chest, but he only regains his hold on her. Their feet moving squarely and awkwardly on the floor, he isn't a great...or even a good dancer. But Sally falls beautifully in his arms...a practiced and perfect fit. Hours pass and they sway and she closes her eyes, glancing up sometimes to find him studying her face.

All day at work she can't think about anything but him. *What a ridiculous ass I am..acting like a young lovebird. Acting like something I don't know I ever was. And I know better...I know it's only show, but it feels so good. Wish I could figure myself out. Talk...I need to talk. Need to hear my voice making sense and get him out of my head...or not. Forget Ralph.*

I already know what he'll tell me. And I really don't want to hear it. I'm not being logical...so what...so what. It's my life. But still...Christ I'm going to explode if I don't talk to someone. No one allows me to feel good anymore. From behind her desk Sally watches Viki pick at some old scotch tape stuck on the countertop.

Waiting to catch her eye, Sally waves at Viki. Eagerly waving back, Viki makes her way to Sally's office in a huff.

"How is it, Viki?"

"Good, good." She looks down at Sally's purse and smiles. "You wanta go outside for a smoke?"

"Sure. You smoking now?"

"Ahh. No. I mean sometimes. But I didn't mean that. I meant you wanta go outside and talk."

"Yeah. Sure. Actually I'd love to."

With a heavy breath, Viki smiles. "Good...Great. I'm so happy."

Sally furrows her brow to try to understand

what's going on. Grabbing her purse, she follows Viki out the door to the soda machine.

Instead of stopping, Viki walks right past Sally's usual spot and sits down at the picnic table under the shade of the old pine tree.

"I thought you might like it here, better. All right, so spill the beans."

"What are you talking about?" asks Sally.

"Come on.   I got ears...it's a small town...and everyone's got eyes. When did he get back into town?"

"Oh...ah...last night. Actually yesterday."

"How is it?"

"What?"

"Come on. You two dancing on the floor, after you almost just about dumped him..."

"Never mind.   I thought...wow...I just thought..."

"What?" Viki eyes Sally with concern.

"Viki...it kinda hurts my feelings to hear that people are talking about me behind my back. Like I'm a walking joke or something."

"Oh my gosh, no. That ain't it at all. In fact it's the opposite. They don't usually talk about you at all -- not that I'm like the height of gossip, but I hadn't ever heard anyone talk you up, except you just seemed like you were done with your man...and then there he was back in your life."

"Yeah? It just is weird that anyone cares."

"Well, they don't. Not the way you mean it...Sally?"

"Yeah?"

"What is it?"

Sally stares down at her fingernails and then digs out her package of cigarettes. "Long story, for sure."

"I ain't going anywhere."

Sally lights her smoke and holds her face still in contemplation. "Well, okay. First I gotta ask you...," she smiles at her own question, "You ever been in love?"

"Sort of...but I...he didn't feel the same...at least he wouldn't say so. But yeah."

"So you know what it feels like...to

long...after something is gone?"

Viki says nothing, but the sadness of her expression tells Sally to continue.

"Last night was about longing. About an empty hole that I can't fill up myself. A place so dark...and you know...untouched...untouchable that I can feel it gurgle sometimes inside me. Like some kind of animal. Or a monster. But I, Christ, sometimes it feels like I can be touched. And I swear to God, he's the only one that makes me feel that way. Like I'm being touched. And I'm so lonely without him."

Sally's eyes well with tears as she picks at the paint on the picnic table with her fingernail. "It's so sad to know that it's him. He's my one. And he's a shit, I know, but I don't know what else to do. I mean what are my options here, right?" Sally laughs and glances at Viki, whose eyes burn into her. "Christ, why you looking at me like that?"

"What if he hurts you again?"

"I won't let him..."

"How?"

"Christ, I just got through telling you that he's the only person that makes me feel alive, and you're telling me...giving me a fucking pep talk."

Pulling back and within herself, Viki sits quiet.

"I don't have a choice here, Viki. I guess I do, but you got to understand what it is to be hollow inside. To feel like you're so rotten through and through that no one else could ever want you, really, anyways. I got two girls who love him...he's their father. What am I supposed to do? Leave him? I can't. It's not in his plans. I don't call the fucking shots and where am I supposed to go? Maybe if I got some stability I could make...if I get this...when I get this promotion I'll be able to piece together a path. But for now...I just miss him. Am I making any sense?"

"Sure," says Viki behind angry, small eyes.

"What's wrong? I'm sorry if I ...I--"

"No. You're fine. Everything is going to work out great for you. Good luck. I better be going." Viki stands up and walks away, leaving Sally alone at the picnic table.

falling

Lying alone in her bed, Sally thinks of David on the couch. Her pores and cells activate themselves in memory of his touch, and she closes her eyes trying to think of anything else. His loud, sleeping breath twists from his nose down the hallway into their bedroom and up through her ears. *He might as well be the God damn pied piper. Shit.* Sally slides herself out from under her sheet, her feet hitting the cool floor. Through the cricket-humming stillness of the night she makes her way down the hall, his breath heavier and louder in the darkness. Fear builds as she approaches, but she no longer controls her feet, and finally she is at the couch. Through the darkness she sees him, and she smiles to herself, he's no prize. No Greek gods in her house. She studies him, feeling safe to look at him and memorize him here in the darkness...where he can't twist things around, make her say and feel things she doesn't mean. Taking two steps backwards, Sally starts to return to the bedroom, but as if controlled by marionette strings her body stops and hangs limp in the hallway. *Why do I always have to be strong? It isn't like I'm not married to the son of a bitch. It isn't like we wouldn't all be happy to get along. Please God, it's just my bed is so empty. I feel so alone...and knowing he's here to fill me...it seems wrong to turn my back to his arms. I just miss him. I don't want anything, but his touch. It's been such a long time since I felt his kindness. And he has been so kind. I just want to be held. Please, understand, God.*

Tears forming in her eyes Sally makes her way to the couch, and small as a little girl she takes her seat at his feet. David stirs and wakes up.

"What?" he says in a gruff voice.

Sally sits motionless at his feet, and he clears his nose and throat of sleep with a big breath. Between them there is silence, and finally her tears become less muted, and her shoulders shake with sadness. Waiting for the right moment, David reaches over and pulls her to him. Holding her on top of him, she cries -- her tears filled with gratitude for his arms and chest. Almost immediately his hand begins to caress her, and make its way over her familiar skin, finally pushing under her underwear onto flesh. His hands yank and pull. Sally's body is frozen and her tears have stopped, but David's breath is heavy and excited. *Just let it be. Just let it be. I'm so fucking tired. This is what you asked for anyway. You can fool yourself, but you can't fool him.*

"So ask Queenie there what's got her so uptight," says David looking at Sally, but directing his question to the girls. Everyone has gathered for breakfast, but Sally has only prepared coffee. "We ain't got shit to eat...and Queenie don't feel like cooking today, anyway. I feel like taking on the world though. Tell ya what!"says David loudly into Sally's ear as he slaps her behind. He laughs.

Sally says nothing, just finds her chair and sips her coffee. David could say anything and she wouldn't care. Today she finds out about the promotion...and after last night no bond exists between them. *I feel nothing for him. He isn't my soul mate...it wasn't about anything special. It was about getting something he wanted and I wouldn't let him have. Never again. This job is mine...and he is out of our lives, once and for all. Please, just let me remember this feeling. He isn't...He's nothing. I deserve so much more.*

"Look at her...well let me tell you something, Queenie...you won't get it!"

Sally snaps out of her thoughts, "What?"

"You won't get it. They want people who have brains to work for them. Just trust me, you won't get it."

Sally stands up and prepares to leave. "You girls catch the bus. I'm going to work. Wish me luck."

Kate and Andrea embrace Sally, and David laughs.

"I'm telling you, you won't get it."

"Bye," says Sally and she's out the door.

Driving to work Sally can't help but feel a foreshadowing of doom...but that's just David's words ringing in her head, she reminds herself. The day is beautiful, and a good distraction...the first hints of autumn in the air, cold and refreshing and full of change. The sage burnt crisply by the morning sun; every possibility is open. She smiles at the truth of possibility, but her nerves form a ball in the pit of her stomach -- heavy, tense, negative, and defeated. All her senses awake from the intensity of her stress, Sally's eyes soak up each sign and every face on Main Street, almost as though everyone is being met for the first time, every storefront being seen for the first time. When she drives onto the parking lot, her insides are on sensory overload, and she floats all the way to the office.

It's already ten thirty when Paul finally motions for Sally to come to his office. By the strained look in his eyes, she knows she should run away and avoid this confrontation. *But I've never been able to read his thoughts before. Why could I tell...now...You're a sure thing, Sally. I think I'm going to vomit.*

"Please...sit down," says Paul with a nervous smile.

Sally sits down, her world crumbling down around her shoulders, like little pieces of dry wall being attacked by giant insects... small and large chunks fly past her...she thinks she can almost visibly see all the stability around her shattering. Originally, she'd been afraid she'd cry, sitting in this room, with Paul having that expression. Instead she feels nothing. A rubber numb.

"Sally, you know this has been hard for us. We've made some real careful consideration..."

Paul's voice begins to sound distant and foreign. Sally watches his lips move, but she can't place meaning with the words. Individually, the words still make sense, but piecing them together isn't   a   possibility. "the...forest...meeting...arrange...job... interviews..."

"I, on a personal level want you to know...that I look forward to you being up for promotion in two years. I think that will have given you time to further enrich your skills...and be ready for that next step. Please know, Sally, we all think you're wonderful, here. We love having you in this, well, how can I put it...family...and that's what you make it feel like...a family. We just want you to have more time to mature, before going to the next level. Keep up the wonderful work...and you're a sure thing next time around. Do you have any questions?"

Sally shakes her head and remains seated in the chair.

"This is so hard for us here..."

Sally smiles and nods. "Yeah..." After a moment of silence she asks, "When does my replacement arrive?"

"Well, we've got the fire crew cleaning up the old Ranger's house, today. By week's end. We just wanted to give her a chance to become situated before the season comes to a close. But we'll be keeping her on year-round. You'll need to show her around the office, orient her with the space here."

With great sadness in her eyes, Sally smiles. "Alright then. Thanks, Paul." And with great effort she rises from the chair and leaves his office.

Entering the front office, Sally's head spins; nothing feels attached to the ground. Through the blurriness, Sally sees Viki's face staring at her, a curious grin in her eyes. Holding herself up straight, Sally focuses all her energy on the back door. Pushing the door open, the transition from interior to exterior overpowers her. Each of her steps heavy and echoing loud, she walks to the fire office. At arrival she stands like a ghost, invisible, looking inside the office. Buck has made his way over from the Helitack base and everyone sits and laughs, while he tells a story.

"So Sky Boner is all in a bunch..because...I can't even remember... I think he wanted me and Simon to wash the dishes, but we didn't want to. And so he keeps on huffing and acting like a moron, and we keep egging him on. Finally, he yells at us, 'Listen some of us aren't pigs...and if you wouldn't mind acting like a human and cleaning up your shit...' So, of course, we say stuff like, 'No wonder your wife divorced you.' And his skin is so red, it's almost blue with anger... Anyway, just before dusk, we get a call to go up to the Lakes. So basically we arrive just in time to set up camp and go to sleep...and we're watching him make a cot in a little corner by himself...folding his little pants into a pillow and fluffing his sleeping bag. So we wait until we hear him sleeping and really quiet, Simon and I pull over a trash can full of garbage, and we leave it about a foot away from his bed. Then we go to bed. Well, at about two, along comes the biggest damn bear you've ever seen to eat some garbage. He's making all this racket and so Sky Boner hearing all the racket, yanks out his little flash light and about five inches from him is this enormous bear head...Boner almost lost his load. He yelled so loud, the bear ran away and every neighbor in a mile's radius knew!...We couldn't stop laughing."

The fire office fills with laughter. Jerry opens his mouth and makes the sound of a crowd cheering, and everyone delights in their laughter even more. Outside Sally stands, concealed by the door jam, wishing for the moment she's in to pass...and knowing something in her is broken. Inside the laughter blares.

She makes her way back to the front office,

and sinks behind her desk. Exposed and vulnerable...the giant insects have almost finished off with fabric of her strength. Ralph comes by after lunch...to wish her well. He won't know about his promotion until the following week.

"I guess I just don't believe them. It should have been yours."

"Well, thanks. Thank you. I'll keep that in mind when I get my... never mind. I shouldn't really talk about...Ralph?"

"Yeah, Sal?"

"How could this happen...I don't know what to do?"

"Just keep going. You'll get it next round."

"I better get to work."

"Sure. Let me know if I can help."

Sally smiles weakly, "You couldn't have done more for me. You're a friend..."

Ralph waves his hand to dismiss her words and leaves. Sally's head sinks into work and the day ticks by. Somehow the area behind her desk feels like a safe zone, compared to the doorway of her house. When six o'clock arrives, it takes minutes for Sally to find the strength in her legs to stand.

A long drive home, but not long enough, Sally drives up the street parallel to her own and parks the Jeep. Sitting in there, the dry, hot air pushing through her window, she lets the tears come. No moisture flows, but her body convulses with the release of her hurt, and the preparation of her arrival home. After an hour has passed and dusk has melted into evening, she jams the gear shift into first and jerks out onto the street. She knows she's not ready to come home...she also knows, she'll never be ready to come home. So she might as well just get it over with.

When she opens the door, they're there in the living room, waiting. On the T.V., she can hear Ponch and John talking about some car hijacker, and the CHiPs' theme music starts to play. And it strikes her how absurd life is.

"You get it?" asks Kate.

Sally shakes her head no, and wills the tears in her eyes to stay put.

David's voice twists into a shrill pitched laugh. "Eeeeiiiii!"

Successfully the fiber of her strength collapses with the shrillness of his glee, and the final chunks of the drywall that once surrounded her core perceptibly fly across the room. Sally sinks to the ground and folds; control lost...floods of tears escape her. The girls rush to her and stand close, not knowing what to do when their mother weeps like this, and David returns his attention to CHiPs, kicking his feet up onto the couch.

With his eyes still on the set he says, "Well, maybe we can get some breakfast made for us sometimes. Huh, girls?"

Kate turns at David and gives him a look of extreme hatred.

After a quick glance, David bursts out in laughter. "You're more like your Mama every day, Katie." After a few minutes of thinking he says, "It's too bad. 'Course it's too bad, Sally. But you just shouldn't have counted on it. You shoulda known it wouldn't come your way...think for once, you know. They had so many people to pick from...Why'd they pick you? You know."

Sally's tears are quieter now, and she thinks she's got the strength to make it to the bedroom. But when she looks and sees Andrea watching her, she weeps again...*How have I done this to you? I am such a failure and you deserve so much better...Your mother is a nothing...a loser...fucking derelict. And I don't know how it happened. Andrea...I'm so sorry.*

"Katie, get me a beer out of the fridge," says David.

By week's end, Sally has moved out of her office -- back to the main office space. A staleness inside her, she waits for the mid-morning to roll around, when her replacement will arrive. By about 10:30 in the morning a U-haul pulls up alongside Main Street. Sally can see the yellow edge of the truck from her window. For about five minutes Sally holds her breath, unsure how to receive her new boss. Finally a small, blond child pries open the office door, allowing an adult female to enter.

The woman, Lori, is hardly one to be jealous of (overweight with grown-out, bleach-blond hair and a bad perm) she enters the office with a heavy weight of guilt riding on her shoulders and neck. Fleshy lines on Lori's face reveal years of drinking and loneliness, and in spite of herself, Sally can't help but be amused by the fact that this person who broke her will is quite possibly even more broken than herself. Sally's gaze drops down to a pale, shy girl, Angie, who clings to Lori's thigh.

"This is the castle...the command tower...if you will," says Sally, pointing to her old office.

"Yeah...looks like it. You cleaned it! Thanks. Angie, let go of me...I can't move." Prying her daughter from her leg, she tells Sally, "You wouldn't believe how often I've moved into a shit hole...no one thinking about how hard it is to move into a mess."

Sally smiles. "That's us. Ship shape and all

that shit." Both women laugh. "I'll get the crew to move in your boxes."

"Oh -- in the U-haul? Those are personal..."

"Okay, I'll take you to the Ranger's house. Now...we cleaned that, and it's still a shit hole."

"I'll be forewarned," says Lori.

"You'll need it."

Sally walks ahead of Lori and Angie, guiding them across the compound to the old house where they'll live. When Sally reaches the Ranger's house, Lori pushes past her and enters the screen door. Watching her stout body enter the house, trailed by ghost-like Angie, Sally identifies herself with them; this burnt-out alcoholic and her defeated daughter are like a reflection, an unkind, and truthful mirror. *This is the path. It is here and now, and it doesn't get any better.* Lightheaded, Sally tries to brace herself on the deteriorating doorway, and watches the sunlight on the back of her hand.

"This really is a dump," yells Lori from inside.

"Yep. Older than this town, I think," replies

Sally.

"Almost as old as I feel..."

Both women explode in an odd laughter, jagged and ugly, almost like witches cackling.

"That makes you a good ten years younger than me," says Sally. Without speaking Lori walks out of the house and back across the compound to the U-haul.

Pushing her cart through Joe's Market, the only market in town, Sally stops at the freezer section. A pool of water collects in the aisle, because the second freezer is broken, defrosting all the T.V. dinners. Sally keeps pushing through the puddle...the next section of freezers hum efficiently and store Golden Creme ice creams, fudgesicles, ice cream sandwiches, big sticks, and drumsticks. Stopping and watching the items on the other side of the glass, Sally takes the lettuce and canned corn and cheese and oatmeal out of her cart and places them on the rack next to her. Opening the freezer door, Sally stands for a few minutes in contemplation and then in a kind of frenzy, she yanks out Mint Chip ice cream, big sticks, ice cream sandwiches -- chipwiches, plain, napoleon, chocolate dipped, and finally a gallon of Rocky Road.

Moe, the town bachelor, opens up his register when Sally approaches the check-out, which is his custom with all the attractive women in town. Embarrassed, Sally places her ice cream on the counter.

"Having a party?" asks Moe.

Relieved, Sally smiles and nods her head yes.

"I just love ice cream. What's the occasion?"

"Nothing," admits Sally with a sheepish smile.

"All the better. You're a woman after my own heart! A party, for the pleasure of living."

"Something like that."

"That'll be nineteen sixty-three." Taking Sally's money, Moe flashes his smile. "You need any help with this stuff...taken to the car?"

"No.   Thanks though.   But I do need a plastic spoon."

Sitting inside her Jeep in the grocery parking lot, Sally pries open the box of ice cream sandwiches and eats one...then another one. She starts to hum, and reaches over, pulling out the Rocky Road, shaving two, big spoonfuls into her mouth. Sally stops eating, almost to gag on the richness. Putting the lid back on the Rocky Road, she reaches for the Mint Chip. The lid pulls off and her eyes absorb the green texture and sad flicks of dark chocolate. Spoon in hand, she digs and stuffs her mouth, digs and stuffs her mouth; with hardly enough time to digest one bite, she puts a new one to her lips. Almost weak from the urgency of loading her mouth, Sally slows down and looks again at the green ice cream, her eyes spilling over with tears. And slowly she shovels more ice cream in her mouth, her cheeks drip wet with large and salty tears.

"Eureka! I've found it," says Sally and she starts to laugh. "All this happiness, just for me." And she laughs and cries and eats ice cream.

After shoving the remainder of the melted and soggy ice cream containers into the dumpster, Sally drives out of the parking lot heading for home. Fall ever approaching, the last of the sun's warmth shines just tipping over the mountains with a hint of nostalgia and the approaching school year. *Kate and Andrea will need to order some new clothes from the Sears catalog...or maybe we should head out of town. We'll catch a movie, or something. Maybe we can do that. But how can I take the time off? I'm too tired anyway...I don't want to be spending hours driving. David won't like it anyway. They can get their God-damn clothes from Sears...and if that isn't good enough...they can just talk to their father. He can discipline them. Somebody else around here can try for once. I just am sick to death of trying and I'm just not going to waste time doing it...no one gives a shit anyway.*

Element of Blank

Sally flicks on her headlights as she turns toward Main Street. The teenagers cruise through, blasting music and wolf whistles and bitchy laughter. The football season has finally arrived. A blond, pretty, thick-waisted girl screams to her girlfriend on the other side of Main Street. BamBam's teems with parents and younger siblings, preparing for the game...joyous and nervous. The words "weekend" and "party time" chant through the small town alleyways, high school gym, and busy restaurants. Waiting a long time for the cruising cars to pass, Sally finally hangs a left and scoots out of town to her den.

Entering the house loudly, in a strange state of defiance, Sally joins David watching T.V., and throws herself down in heavy fatigue. Unmoving, her eyes glue to the news broadcast, David kicks his big, spoiled sock feet onto her lap. Sitting at the kitchen table, Kate and Andrea draw unicorns, and pretty girls with big, brilliant eyes. David pinches Sally's thighs with his toes, but she doesn't look at him.

"What are we having to eat? Didn't you go shopping?" says David.

"Yeah. I don't care. Make anything. Katie!"

"Yeah?"

"Make dinner tonight. You're always aching to be Chef Boy Are Dee...now's your chance."

"But... I don't..."

"Fine. I don't care. We're having popcorn."

David laughs and watches Sally study the television set. Heading for the kitchen, he gets up, takes a spoon from the dish rack and grabs a jar of peanut butter out of the refrigerator. Sucking on the spoon he returns to the sofa, plops down mimicking Sally's fatigue, laughs at his joke and grabs the remote control, surfing through the four stations their antenna receives. With absolute concentration and her front teeth biting her lip, Kate now has taken out her felt-tip marker set and traces the unicorn's horn with yellow ink. Transfixed, Andrea studies Kate's artistic mastery.

Element of Blank

Sally remains still...unaffected and unaware of her own existence; as completely turned off as the on-off button on the T.V. set.

After an hour, Sally gets up and puts a bag of popcorn in the microwave. She turns the dial to five minutes and walks to the bathroom. The timer on the microwave dings, the toilet flushes, and Sally walks back into the kitchen. Pouring the mildly burnt popcorn into two bowls, Sally places one at the table with Andrea and Kate, and brings the other into the living room. Setting the bowl on the coffee table, she collapses into the couch and doesn't move again. Her limbs limp and lifeless, she watches the set with its flashing images. And now everyone ignores her, as well. There is the quiet hum of indifference. The evening rolls into night, which rolls into sleep, which turns into escape.

In a state of sadness time can slow down so much that it disappears. Nothing to define the difference from one day to the next. Unable to exist in the present, because of the overpowering state of despair, hours can be weeks and a month can easily be a year. Waking on a Saturday, three weeks after her demotion, Sally sees the paint on the bedroom wall. And because it has been such a long time since she'd noticed anything, she wonders if she's ever really looked at that wall...wonders if she has ever really invested any pleasure in knowing it. Indeed, she tells herself she never has. Waking from her sleep, the twisted path of her life sets in front of her thoughts. *So, so much the same. Every peak only exists to pave the way for a new depth. Every cycle, is just that. A path back to the beginning. Who am I kidding? I will always travel so far just to arrive back here. And this time...I don't have the strength to scale out of the pit. My God...I really don't think I have the ability to get out of this.*

Looking around her, the wall's brightness which had first caught her eye seems to warp and turn gray. The roof above her feels heavy and crushing. With a heavy, sinister raspiness, David begins to snore beside her. Wanting like a child to pull the covers over her head, she lies motionless, paralyzed by fear. Everything her pupils find turns from happy to ugly, bright to broken. Closing her eyes, she prays just to see nothing and protect what remains. Behind closed lids flash pictures of Andrea into her mind, and she quickly unshuts her eyes in search of something as yet untouched by her gaze. Anything to distract her mind from the girls.

Looking, looking, her eyes find the archway to the door, and the sunlight shushes away while she stares. And now time for something else to find...anything else. Pulling herself out of bed, Sally enters the hallway, her eyes soaking in the false wood paneling, putrefying it and moving on. The kitchen, soaked up and spit out...the living room...soaked in and spit out...

Behind her stirs small feet, and afraid, Sally won't turn around.

"Mom?" asks Kate, with concern.

"Go back to bed."

"What?"

"Now!" yells Sally. And when the feet have quietly moved away back to the bedroom, Sally finds her way to the kitchen table, and cries while she stares at the ugliness of her own hands.

"Hey, did you want to come, too, Sally? End of the season trip to the Mexican restaurant up to the Lakes. Margaritaville?" asks Morgan P.

"Maybe," says Sally.

"Well, it's on Friday night...be there or be square," and he's out the door. After three seconds Morgan P. returns and looks at Sally, her desk in the middle of the common area, "Can we talk?"

"I'm really pretty busy."

"It's about this," says Morgan P. motioning to the office, letting his eyes deliberately fall on Lori inside her office and make their way back to Sally.

"I don't really want to talk about it."

"It's about Ralph."

"What?"

"Can we talk outside?"

"Fine...sure. Let me grab my smokes." After reaching for her purse, Sally follows Morgan P. outside. She snaps her lighter and plunges the cigarette into the flame. Dragging in and out, then in and out with Morgan P.'s eyes on her, she finally asks, "Well, don't just stand there. Spit it out."

"Ralph got passed by, too. They kept putting it off. This morning he found out. Maybe you could talk to him. He's so upset. Becky's coming down, but the kids are sick...he doesn't want to talk to me...I figured you could...talk to him better than any of us, anyway."

"Right," says Sally as she sucks on her smoke, distractedly thinking. "Thanks...I'll go right now." Taking a final puff, Sally flings the cigarette onto the ground. As she looks up from staring at the cigarette butt on the cement, Morgan P. smiles at her. Turning away from him, Sally walks to the fire office.

Everyone away on different projects, Ralph and Stan sit together in the office, their desks and backs turned away from each other. With a knock on the door, Sally enters.

"Hey Sal. Ain't been seeing much of you these days."

"Nope. How you been, Stan?"

"Yeah...same. Yourself?"

"Been better...tell you the truth. But okay."

Stan nods his head and Sally's eyes move from his face to the back of Ralph's head. "Hey you...got any time for a stranger?"

Ralph turns around and says, "For you, stranger, I always got time." He stands up from his chair and walks toward the doorway. "I'll be right back, Stan."

"Take your time. Not like the barn's burning or something," replies Stan, not lifting his head from the paperwork on his desk.

Making their way to the asphalt outside the fire office, Ralph points Sally to the football field. "Let's play a little bit of hooky."

Sally smiles.

Walking along, Ralph talks about his anger and his feelings of betrayal. Sally nods and agrees, sometimes adding feelings of her own. But mainly she walks without listening to Ralph, only knowing what he's saying by the tone of his voice. After completing the track twice through, they hear Becky's voice calling for Ralph.

"She's here," says Sally.

"Hum, okay...Strange. Sally, I'm ashamed to go to her."

"She...she's not that kind of person. You shouldn't be."

"Yeah, I guess."

They walk in silence. And when they open the gate to the compound, Becky stands with the baby strapped to her body, her hair disheveled and her face full of worry, waiting.

"Sorry it took so long...Mom and Dad are driving to Swansee today...so I just took Sammy and Wade to town with me." Walking up to Ralph she kisses his cheek. "How are you?"

"Fine. Damn bastards."

"Hi, Sally. I'm so sorry that you didn't get promoted...either. It isn't right."

Sally smiles at Becky. "Listen, I better get back. You two have got lots to talk about. Nice seeing you, Becky. Sorry Ralph." Walking away as far as the picnic table Sally secretly glances at them behind her. She watches as Becky removes the baby from its carrier and hands him to Ralph, their bodies moving in close together and Becky's head lowers and balances on Ralph's shoulder.

"All right, this is bullshit!" says David. "I've been more than fair with you. But you don't ever...and I mean fucking ever touch my shit without asking me first. You understand?"

Baked and glassy eyed, Sally makes no reaction, sitting outside on the lawn chair.

Kicking the lawn chair so that it collapses onto the ground, causing Sally to bounce as her body strikes the surface, David yells, "Do you get it? Fat ass."

Letting out a wild scream, Sally forms the word, "Yes."

"Jesus." And David enters back into the

house.

Her pupils dilated, Sally lets the autumnal sun bake on her skin...and the numbness fills her. Laying on the collapsed lawn chair, the silent mountains open their mouths and speak to her in mild, muted tones. They don't say anything...just speak like a crazy man talking through a plastic bag. Way far away the traffic speeds along the highway. Copying the noises, Sally moves her lips and laughs and hums and twists the muted mountain noises from her mouth and makes the pitter patter of the automobile wheels hitting the asphalt.

death

The end. How can one explain it? And the what and the why of it? Suddenly does life ring cleaner and clearer as death moves its way through the little town and taps on your door? No. Probably not, at least. A day is a day is a day. When one wakes on the day of her death, from the final sleep of her life...it's just the beginning of another day in the crazy chain of days that link together to form an existence.

Pasty-mouthed and face molded into her pillow, Sally's eyes flicker open. Squeeze tight. Force out daylight. Opening suddenly, her eyes focus onto the alarm clock. Wanting to jump out of bed, her arms just stay, pushed and tucked under her body.

"No," she says.

David moans beside her.

Rolling her face over the pillow to look at him, to try to tell him she can't get out of bed, Sally becomes aware that she wears only a t-shirt with no underwear. *Fuck...I don' t ...how. Son of a Bitch, bastard. You couldn't just let me be? Prick...Christ, I've got to get up. I've got to get up. Get up. GET up. What's wrong with me? The shithead. I have to get up. But I can't. What the fuck's he -- Pervert. Asshole. Why can't I move? I'll just lay here instead. Since I can't goddamn move. Be very, very quiet.* Sally laughs as she makes the voice of Elmer Fudd in her mind and David hisses out a moan. *So, so sorry to disturb you, sleeping fucking beauty.*

"Sorry," mumbles Sally.

David moans again.

"Shhhh!" she says.

David moans and pushes against Sally.

"Shhhh!"

An angry eye flashes open in David's face, and he growls. "Shut!" Half in his dream he shoves her right out of bed, her head knocking against the night stand. Sally lays there on the floor, looking up at the ceiling, her T-shirt vulnerably hiked up her body, exposing her nakedness and frozen limbs. With an angry roll over onto his stomach, David slips back into his sleep.

Sally raises her head and peers down over her flesh, looking to the end of her body. Tears fill up Sally's eyes, and her throat constricts. *I am not going to do this. I just need to get out of here. Control. Focus. Knock it off. Don't be a pussy. Little baby -*

knock it off. Focus. If I could only move my feet. I'll start with them. Come on. Please, please. Yes! Good. I'm going to get out of here. Now for you little bastards. Move. I'm doing this. Legs next. Just up and go. There we go. I'm fucking doing it. Thank you very much. Just through there to the bathroom. That's it. A delicious shower. That'll get me pumping. Just get up to the shower. Just to the shower. Come on, now. You can do it. Ouch. Come on. Come on you bastard. Get up. Now. Work body. Up. UP. UP. And she is standing. Stumbling toward the door, she grabs ahold of the doorway.

David groans vaguely out of his dreams.

Moving down the hallway, Sally braces herself into the bathroom. At the edge of the bathtub she balances her body and turns on the faucet. She pulls off her t-shirt, and wraps her arms over her chest. Water pouring out, and once the heat has built up, she pulls the spigot and the warm water fans out from the showerhead. Teetering on one shaky foot, she climbs into the tub. Her back to the warm water, Sally lets it pound into her skin as she sinks down into the tub, folding her body and kneeling so far that her chin rests on her own knees and her forehead rubs on the plastic grip strips at the bottom of the bath tub. The warm water travels into her mouth, draining from the back of her neck, and she spits in order to breathe. Meditation and return to the womb. Minutes slip by and add up until all the hot water is gone.

Rubbery, but much more functional, Sally's legs contort and raise her up. Shutting the water off, Sally squats back down into the tub, resting on her back this time, her arms spanning the rim of the tub. Gaining composure and strength, Sally remains motionless; the wetness of her body becomes cold, but she remains in the bathtub.

With bloodshot eyes and angry tension, David enters the bathroom. Shielded by the beveled shower door, Sally can only see David's back as he urinates into the toilet.

"I wasn't wearing any underwear."

"Yeah."

"Why?"

"I don't know." There is a pause while David concentrates on peeing. As he shakes away the urine, he clears his throat and says, "You were hoping to get lucky? You tell me."

"Pig," says Sally, with a quiet rage, her eyes focusing toward the spigot in the bath tub.

David turns around and looks at Sally laying nude in the tub. He laughs. "Ain't nobody else'd fuck you, that's for sure. Look at you. Goddamn cow...look at your ass piling up and spilling every fucking where. Mooo. Moooo." David moos right over Sally's voice.

"Well, I don't mind it."

"Moooo. MOOO."

"...And I don't want you touching it."

"MOOOOO."

David bursts into a huge laugh. "Shit. You are too, too much. Fine, fine. Rot away. Bitch," utters David under his breath while he exits the bathroom leaving the door wide open. "Good Morning to you, too," he says from the hallway.

Element of Blank

Running her fingertip over the bubbles of water that line the walls of the tub, Sally begins to trace a picture. First a flower, then she draws a home, with windows like eyes and smoke puffing out the chimney. Drinking in the picture, Sally follows the lines over and over with her eyes. In the kitchen David slams open and shut the cabinet doors. Her eyes still study the lines of her imaginary home, and a tremor forms in Sally's bottom lip. Taking her fingertip, Sally traces letters on the shower door, F....U....C....K....Y....O...U. A strange triumph and sadness form into a little laugh, and Sally stands up, grabs a towel, and walks into the kitchen, her hair wet, sticking to the back of her neck.

"Eggs? Or you want a sandwich? It's almost lunch."

"Why aren't you at work?"

"I was sick...and I couldn't stand. What do you want?"

"I don't care."

Sally opens the refrigerator and takes out

butter and a carton of eggs. The eggs whisk together with a fork, and pour over melted butter in an aluminum skillet. A quiet hiss of cooking eggs and Sally's fork dragging over the aluminum pan. Setting down the plate in front of David, she goes to the phone.

"Hi. It's Sally. I'm really ill. Sorry, I didn't call. I couldn't get to the phone. Could you tell Lori for me? I'm feeling better now...so if you need me to, I can come in to work after lunch...Yeah...Thanks... No, yeah...I'm at home...Where else would I be...I'm sick...Very funny. Thank you. 'Bye now."

"Who the fuck was that? Your new boyfriend?"

"What do you care?"

"I don't."

"It was Ralph. He didn't get the promotion, either."

"Like I said. They've got bigger fish to fry then the bunch of losers in this town."

Saying nothing, Sally walks back to the

bedroom, still sticky and pungent with last night's sleep, and the stale odor of sex. She puts on jeans and a T-shirt and lays down on the bed. Humming quietly at first, then the notes and words come softly, "Amazing grace, how sweet the sound to save a wretch like me...was lost, but now I'm found...Oh amazing grace...was blind, but now I see" Laying very still, Sally's eyes follow the fragments and lines in the structure. Ceiling becomes wall becomes window becomes wall becomes new wall becomes doorway. Shutting her eyes the visual imprint still rings under her lids, and lines flash and shine and jut across, forcing beams and jail iron to trap into her brain as Sally drifts into a new sleep.

After about five minutes, the pressure of a light weight on the bed makes Sally stir. Then the soft child's smell lightly dancing from Andrea's hair fills Sally's nose. Curling herself up, Andrea nests into Sally's stomach. Breathing her in, enjoying her grace, Sally doesn't move. They both drift off into sleep. Within a few minutes, Sally wakes up and shakes Andrea's shoulders.

"Why aren't you at school?"

"What?" asks Andrea in a confused tone.

"Why are you here! You should be at school."

"But...there isn't school. It's summer."

"Of course there's school...summer school."

"No. Um...it's over. Until real school."

"What are you talking about?" Sally looks accusingly at Andrea's face. "You better not be lying. You lying? If I find out you're lying, I'll slap your butt - silly. You hear me?"

"Yeah."

Letting go of Andrea's face, Sally breaks away from her little girl. "Good."

And then there is the silence and the awkward end of the tenderness preceding the fight. Sally lies awake on her back, her eyes on the ceiling and Andrea creates an imaginary force field between herself and her mother. Outside, the Harley barks and roars, finally backing out of the driveway, leaving the little women together again.

"Jesus Christ," says Sally. "Won't this God-damn day ever end? If I'm not doing one thing wrong, it's another."

"I don't think you're wrong, Mom," says Andrea quietly.

"Shut up, now. 'Course I'm wrong. Been wrong so long...I am just wrong, naturally." Sally laughs and yanks at Andrea's blond hair, loosely braiding it, while they both watch the wall. "Love you, nut."

"Love you, Mom."

For another half hour they rest like this, laying on their sides, nuzzled into each other, facing the wall, allowing their minds to think of nothing. Outside the sound of dry wind snapping through the sage brush and grabbing and scattering dusty dirt builds rapidly. Rattling against the window screens, the wind knocks to come in...flinging little sand piles into the bedroom. The gusts increase their intensity and soon the feebleness of the house seems to shake in the wind.

Getting out of bed to shut the window, Sally

stands up and looks outside. Just beyond the bedroom window, between a field of blowing tumbleweeds and shaking sage brush stands Kate. Her hair blowing and twisting in the winds, Kate bows down her face to protect herself from the wind. Taking her hands to make goggles for her eyes, Kate brings her head back up and continues balancing herself on an imaginary tightwire. Her clothes flap in conflict with her body and the wind...Kate keeps her head high with hands enveloping her eyes, as she passes to the other end of the invisible rope bobbing her body gracefully, against all odds, to the place of safety beyond the imaginary cheering crowds and competitive, evil opponents. Sally sees Kate make it to safety, watches her with intuitive respect, and love, and separation.

"You hungry, Andrea?" asks Sally with her eyes still focused outside on Kate in the wind.

"Yeah-huh."

"Well, then don't just lay there. Get up and make me something to eat."

Andrea looks at her mother with utter shock. Turning her head, Sally tries to look indignant, but only brims over with laughter when she sees the appalled look on Andrea's face.

"Hey, Smart Alec -- How many times I made you make lunch for me? Jeez." Sally smiles. "Go outside and get your sister. She'll blow away out there. And tell her lunch'll be ready in about twenty minutes."

"'Kay."

Heading for the kitchen, Sally walks out of the bedroom, leaving Andrea as she rolls out of bed. Stretching her arms in front of herself, with catlike flexibility, Andrea makes her way down the hall. Passing Sally digging through the refrigerator, Andrea opens the kitchen door, which the wind sucks from her hand and the interior of the house gasps as the outside winds suck Andrea into the backyard. Trying to run to Kate, Andrea falls down on her knees. Wanting to raise up again the winds shift pushing so hard that she only falls back down.

Laughing, with her hair whipping around her face, Kate walks to Andrea, and offers her a hand up.

"I think you might fly away, Andrea!" yells Kate with a sandy smile and slits for eyes. "Maybe we should go back inside?"

Nodding her head in agreement, Andrea keeps her focus on the ground while holding her long hair with her hands. Kate extends her hand and grabs Andrea's forearm and together they make the final steps back to the kitchen, pulling with all their might to get the door to shut, until finally it slams shut on their faces with a boom.

Sally jumps as she finishes making peanut butter and jelly, tortilla sandwiches. "My God, look at you. Katie. You look like something out the bible...a what's it -- prophet, or a crazy person. All the dust on your face. Look at your hair. We'll never get those Rats' nests out. I'll buy some of that No More Tangles stuff at the drug store tomorrow. Look at you. You must be crazy."

Kate stares at Sally, without a word.

"Well, here's lunch. Wash first. Please." Sally points down the hallway past the two plates on the table, then grabs her plate and heads to the T.V., where she kicks up her feet and watches General Hospital and licks the jam that spills over the edge of the p.b. and j. burrito. The girls finish their food and file into the living room and sit down on the couch with Sally. The wind outside blows the antenna, causing grainy reception sometimes so bad, Sally switches channels for a few minutes, checking back until the reception returns. Lying on the floor, the girls balance on each other's feet, and practice being shot into the air by their buttocks, sometimes crashing into the couch or the wall. After four hours of television, the sun begins to set behind the great, granite mountains and the winds die down to a whisper.

"Go outside for a while and get rid of that energy. You're making me crazy, you. Hyperactive nutballs."

"Fine, mother," says Kate sharply, as she instantly storms out of the house with Andrea lingering slowly behind her.

Stretching herself out on the sofa, Sally turns the volume down on the television set and listens to Kate's voice explain a game to Andrea. Andrea acts as though she already knows the rules and they begin to fight, but the argument subsides and they begin with another game. In the distance, Sally hears David's Harley making its way towards home. Turning the volume back up on the television, Sally braces herself for his return.

The door opens up and David walks in slowly. His hair and skin are twice as dusty as Kate's, and his wide grin exposes shockingly white teeth beneath the dust. David walks to the sink, clears his throat, and spits into the drain. Looking outside at the girls playing in the evening dust David laughs.

"They got a bit of me in them after all. Not sitting on their asses...anyway." His face turns to Sally and he studies her. "That was about the most fun I've had in years. Wind ripping through the tires. My bike wanted to dance all on its own, but I kept her from flipping. Holding the front of her steady, while the back tire skidded to the shoulder and then back to the yellow line. Went out on the dry lake bed. Fell finally, out there. Just laying flat on my back looking at the dust flying a million miles an hour over my face. The sky was brown with dust. A thick, brown cloud about an inch from my eyes, but not touching. You want to go out to eat?"

Sally looks at David with amazement and then lowers her gaze. "Okay. Yeah, sure," she says staring absently at David's dusty pants and boots.

"Sal, you wouldn't believe how fucking hard it was to pick that damn bike up. I must of laid looking at the sky...at least an hour."

"That's great. I'm glad for you."

"Forget it. Forget I said anything," says David as he goes to the bathroom. Sally can hear him urinate, and then his foot steps returning to the living room. "Well, get off your ass. Let's go."

"Sure. I gotta get Katie and Andrea. If that's okay."

"No! Fuck, what am I supposed to say? Well get 'em. Shit. I'm hungry and we don't have crap around here..." Sally goes to the door and calls for the girls while David continues, "Because you're too Goddamn lazy. I should get one of them signs, 'Wide Load' made up for you. Like a t-shirt or something. Maybe a big patch for your ass." Laughing with a hint of warmth and a loud boom, David walks up to Sally at the door and kisses the side of her face as the girls enter from outside. "And that way, won't nobody expect nothing out of you, baby. You're my baby." David grabs Sally's crotch through her blue jeans, and yanks her up against his body. "You're my baby. Don't ever forget it."

"I won't. I promise," says Sally her eyes cold and facing the desert landscape. "I'll never forget what you are to me."

Releasing his hand from her crotch, David sets his head on the back of Sally's neck, and brushes his hand over her breast with a gentle tug of ownership. "Well, let's go. I'm sick of waiting for you." Turning on his heels, David heads out the front door, followed by the girls. Her eyes brimming with tears, Sally takes a deep breath in, and a short exhale. A tension coming to her jaw, the tears disappear, and Sally makes her way to the front door. They wait for her in the Jeep, David sits in the driver's seat. Jumping inside, she hands him the keys and the Jeep flies into town pulling into a parking space outside BamBam's.

Sliding into the red vinyl booth, they are a family. Unmistakably a husband, a wife, and the product of their love, two children. They do not speak. Sally sees their reflection cast in the window. She glances around the restaurant to make sure the reflection is not of another, truer, happier family. It is her family. This public reflection makes her happy. She looks at David with loving eyes, and he makes his gaze shoot coldly right past her face to the back wall of the restaurant.

"What do you girls want?" asks Sally.

Kate shakes her head, "Something. I don't

know."

"How about you, Andrea?"

"What do you call it?"

"A cheeseburger...not booger! Are you retarded or something?" whispers Kate.

"Mom! Kate said I was retarded."

Sally doesn't react to Andrea, but continues studying her menu. Looking around the restaurant, David sees a squinty-eyed teenage girl looking over at his table.

"'Cause you are," says Kate.

"Nah huh! You're retarded."

"Oh, okay. I'm retarded. Who spells "to" backwards? Retard!"

Not looking up from the menu, Sally says, "Enough. Button it...or you're going outside to the Jeep."

"But Mom, Kate--"

"Andrea!"

Standing up, David walks out of the restaurant and gets into the Jeep. The tires squealing on the ground, he peels onto the highway and heads toward home. Sally stares speechless watching him depart, and the girls look at each other, while most of the heads turn their faces toward Sally for a quick glance at her humiliation.

"Girls, get up."

"But Mom. We didn't get to eat," says Kate.

"Girls, now. Up."

"But I'm hungry," says Andrea.

"Now. I don't have any God-damn money. Get up."

With great humility the girls slide out of the vinyl booth and rise to their feet. Standing up, Sally says, "Alright. We'll get food at home."

Andrea says, "But we don't have--" Kate hits Andrea across the back of the head. "OUCH!"

"Well, shut up. Jeez."

"Stop it, girls."

Walking out of the restaurant, Sally and the girls make their way through the town as the lights begin to flicker on, and the sky begins to deepen its shade of blue. Crossing to the west sidewalk, they continue through Main Street until they reach the park with its well-watered grass, flimsy gazebo, and miniature stream. Veering off the road (because the sidewalk has ended) they cut through the park, through the tennis courts, and into the sage brush beyond the little league ball park. In the semi-black of a moonless night, the three make their way through the large field of sage brush and ground hugging cacti outside their back kitchen door. In the distance, babies of the mother coyote yap and howl, seeking out their mother, waiting for her return from the darkness. The ground stacks unevenly beneath their feet with sandy earth and large, porous, volcanic rock, making it difficult for them to keep balance. The only sound for a long time is their breath, the sound of the feet striking the ground, and the childish howls of the baby coyotes. Finally the lights from their neighbor's window can be seen, and the darkness of their own house observed. With their eyes wandering around them, always returning back to their house, they continue walking through gravelly dirt, their feet winding amongst desert plants, mildly scented in the nighttime air: whook, whook, wak, whook, wak, whook, whook, wak, whook...until finally they are walking up to the collapsed lawn chair outside the kitchen door, their faces reflecting the light from the neighbor's bright window.

They enter the house, and David sits in the dark on the couch.

"Girls, go to bed. I'll make you something to eat later."

Without any of their normal complaints, the girls file into the bedroom, as Sally flips on the kitchen light. "Why did you do that?"

"What?" asks David.

"Fucking leave us. That's what."

"You embarrass me. So I left. What's the problem?"

"Fuck you, is the problem. We're human. Christ. Why?"

Making no response, David sits with his back to Sally and the kitchen light. She stands her ground, waiting for him to attack her, and after the tension has fallen slightly from the air David speaks.

"What do you think you're doing?" with a threat in his voice.

"That's rich. Nothing." And after a pause, Sally adds, "Kicking you out of this house. Once and for all."

David howls with laughter. "How you going to do that, Queenie? Pick me up? Or ask me pretty please?"

"How about tell you?"

The laughter stops and David gets to his feet. Turning to face Sally he says, "Don't forget who you're talking to."

Fear betraying her, Sally says nothing, attempting to keep her feet planted firmly to the ground. She raises her chin in defiance.

"Oh that's good. You're good at acting the victim, standing up for your rights...for your whatever fucking beliefs. Too bad you're such a fucking loser." Moving into the kitchen, David opens a drawer and extracts a baggy full of drugs from the back of it. Raising his eyebrows up and down he says, "For a blow job, you can have a couple."

Glaring at him, Sally attempts to walk past him. He lunges over and grabs her by her hair. Pulling her behind toward his lap he falls hard onto the ground. Laughing, David grabs Sally's breast. "What's the matter, baby? Sometimes it makes you so hot. Makes you all wet. Let's just see if --"

"Shut the fuck up. Do it...if you're going to, fucking do it. Just shut up about it," says Sally quietly and full of rage, trying to protect herself from his exploring hands.

Slapping her in the face, "Don't forget who you're talking to."

"I can't."

Throwing her off his lap, David grabs the back of Sally's head and yanks her back to the ground. Sally lays on her back. With a powerful angry fist, David punches down on her left eye. Sally's head bounces off the ground like a rubber ball and slams back down. She is motionless. Pulling back, David sits down on the chair, reaches down and picks up the baggy. Tossing a couple pills in his mouth, he shakes his head back and swallows. Looking at her chest raise and fall, David sits.

Minutes pass and his senses begin to numb themselves as the drugs kick into action. Standing up David towers over Sally. Serenity surrounds her angelic face; the bruise just a mild violet around her eye, the spidering of ruptured blood in her eye not evident through her closed lids, her mouth lightly shut, her expression peaceful. Pulling out his penis David urinates on her. Beginning with Sally's stomach his stream follows its way to her face. The warm liquid makes her move her head and hands, but not enough to gain total consciousness. He laughs at her ineffectiveness, as the stream of his urine dies out. Turning his back to Sally, David swaggers to the couch where he throws himself down and studies the shapes his drugs allow him to understand.

Element of Blank

Within an hour Sally becomes conscious. Her one eye opens, the other swollen shut with blood and puffiness, and her nose breathes in the reek of David's piss. Laying on her back, she brings her hand to her inflated face and throbbing head. Finally raising up, she pulls her urine soaked t-shirt over her head, moaning quietly at the pain of pulling the collar over her face. Tossing the t-shirt in the kitchen sink, Sally makes her way to the bathroom in her bra and jeans. Turns on the shower. Climbing inside, she eases shut the shower door. Water spraying all over her pants, she removes the rest of her clothes with the water rushing over her. Shutting off the water, she shakes with the cold, her petite and nude frame exposed. Stepping outside the shower, Sally dries herself off and enters the kitchen wrapped in a towel. Her body prickles from the chill of the midnight air.

After opening a can of corn, Sally turns on the front burner. Searching out a clean pan, she empties out the canned corn and sets the pan on the burner.

"Why don't you wear your clothes?" asks David.

"Some asshole pissed on them," replies Sally, staring down at the corn with a spoon in her hand.

David laughs. "Take your towel off."

"Fuck you."

"Do it."

Sally flips David off. He laughs.

"You want corn?"

"I want some loving."

"Do you want corn?"

"No."

Sally pours the corn into two bowls, grabs two spoons, and walks to the girl's bedroom. Inside she can hear them sleeping together in Andrea's bed. Sally sets the two bowls of corn on Kate's bed, stops herself, retrieves them and walks out of the bedroom holding the two bowls of steaming corn.

Setting the corn on the counter, Sally stands

motionless. Pausing in unthinking, numb silence, she begins to pour the corn over her urine covered t-shirt.

"What you doing. We ain't made of money...Those girls wouldn't eat it! What do they think we are! KATE! ANDREA! Get your asses out here."

"They're sleeping. It's after midnight. They're asleep."

"Now. Don't make me get you out of that bedroom. NOW!" booms David's voice down the hallway. He jumps to his feet and storms toward the girls' bedroom.

Jumping to stop him Sally says, "Damn-it, David. Stop. They didn't--."

David pushes Sally onto the floor.

"You shit. You shit!," screams Sally, sitting on the floor as she hears David crashing down the hallway. The door opens. Paralyzed with fear, Kate and Andrea lay with their eyes wide open. David yanks Kate out of bed and Andrea shrieks and cries.

"Daddy, no," cries Andrea.

Pulled up against her father's side, Kate whimpers with terror as David escorts her through the house, back to the kitchen. Following behind, Andrea stops at the end of the hallway and watches her father thrust Kate's face into her mom.

"You say you're sorry to your mother."

"I'm sorry," says Kate in a cracked voice, tears streaming down her face. Looking up at the bruise on her mother's face, Kate's tears plunge more strongly from her eyes and her face peels into a bright red with little teeth exposed in a pained expression. "I'm sorry," she says again.

"See, Sal. That's the only way to make them mind." Grabbing the tangled dusty mess of Kate's hair, "What is this shit? Jesus. Don't you brush your hair? We're just going to have to cut that off."

"No!" exclaims Kate shrilly. "Mom, make him stop. Please. Stop."

Defeated and terrified, Sally watches as David pulls out his long, sharp pocket knife. "David, no."

Taking all her hair in one lump David cuts twisting the knife back and forth, right close to her skull. The wad of hair falls to the ground, and as Kate's eyes discover the cutting, she howls uncontrollable.

"Oh, shut up. Take care of your hair. If you cared so much, you'd have brushed it."

Getting up from the floor, Sally finds her way across the kitchen. Settling into a chair, she folds her head down, weak from lack of fight and hope, and begins to sob on the table.

Surrounded by weeping faces, David demands, "Well, go to bed. God-damn babies. I'm just taking care of you...cause you don't take care of yourself."

On unsteady feet, Kate stands up and walks past Andrea. They make their way, tears swelling their throats, to their bedroom. The door shut behind them, they climb into Andrea's bed, Kate's hand feeling the strange absence of hair at the back of her neck and the base of her skull.

"Baby," says David. "Don't be so sad.

She's okay."

"It's over."

"No, it ain't. I get to decide that. I mean Christ. It'll grow back." Sally continues to cry, her head resting in her hands. "Lighten up. I didn't hurt her. Here. Have one of these. Here."

Still crying, Sally begins to mumble. "No. How did this happen? You promised me to stop hurting me...I can take it...They can't...they didn't ask for this life...You...you can't hurt them. No. I can take it...you can't touch them. No. No."

"I didn't. Jesus H. Christ. Have this and shut up!!!," shouts David. Grabbing out a couple pills, David pulls Sally's head up by her hair and jams the pills into her mouth. Shutting her jaw down tight on his hand, Sally attempts to tear through David's skin. Forcing his hand further into her mouth, he jerks Sally's head back and yanks his bleeding hand out of her mouth. After she spits the pills out onto the table, David grabs Sally's shoulder and throws her onto the ground, her back whacking onto the linoleum. The air flat from her lungs, David punches her in the eye. Again. Before she can scream in agony, Sally faints from pain...her bath towel loosely wrapped around her small body. A mass upon the floor, he kicks her a couple times in her gut, while he holds a kitchen towel over his hand. Her body reflexes automatically.

For four hours, Sally lays unconscious. At the end of the first half hour, David takes three more pills and turns on the T.V. At four thirty, the late, late movies are over, and the color bars fill the screen. David watches the bars for a while, checks out his wounded hand and flexes the bruise which follows the bridge of Sally's teeth wrapping around his palm into the fresh crust of blood on top of his hand. And then he goes over to Sally. He watches her, her face swollen and purplish. Then he taps her face. When she doesn't react, he fills up a tall glass of water, and then pours it over her face. As she stirs her way awake, David leaves for the bedroom. Returning with his leather biker jacket and Sally's bright blue ski jacket, he picks her up and sets her in the chair.

"There we go. Let's go for a ride. Put this on."

Sally's head falls forward, and she half slips back into unconsciousness. Pulling Sally to her feet and into his chest, David attempts to put her inside the jacket. Her arms limp, the coat keeps almost slipping to the ground, her towel unwrapping off her body.

"Help, God-damn it. Help. You piece of shit."

Her eye rolling open, Sally pulls her arm muscles toward herself, holding the towel to her body. David drapes the coat around her. Carrying her outside into the deep darkness, and cold predawn he sets her into the passenger seat. She starts to slide down onto the floor of the Jeep, and he slaps her cheek, tender with the bruise. "Get up. Get up," he whispers. And he jumps into the driver's seat.

The crisp cold biting his lips and cheeks, and counteracting the numbness of the drugs,

David drives to the highway, turns left and starts heading out of town. Sally's eye blinks open, unfocused and groggy. The early morning air wraps around their faces and they roar past the aqueduct onto the northern towns. Her head nodding forward, and then being nipped by the wind, Sally shifts back and forth from consciousness. Halfway to nowhere, David stops the Jeep and swings it around the other direction. At five forty, just as they make their way back to the outskirts of town, the mountain light shoots over the crests and dawn slowly inches its way toward the valley floor. Instead of returning home, David turns left onto the road which leads to the dry lake beds.

Speeding to a stop in the middle of the flat and dust-cracked earth, David jumps out of the jeep. He pulls Sally out of the vehicle. She falls down on the ground, and doesn't move. "Get up! God-damn, you. GET UP!!!" Sally lays on the dirt. "Fine. Suit yourself." David moves away from the Jeep and sits down. Laying on his back he watches the morning sun warm its way over the mountains. The air warms and the sky brightens, his eyes blink slowly and with contentment. Sitting up, he sees a coyote scamper over the dry lake bed, heading away from the town into the desert mountains. Jumping to his feet, he grabs a rock. He pitches the rock , but it misses and skips off the lake bed, while the coyote runs away with skittish, quick feet.

Turning to Sally, resting in a heap next to the Jeep, he walks to her. One of her arms stuck into the sleeve of the coat and the other free, he tosses her into the passenger's seat. In the early morning brightness, they make their way back across the dry lakes, and back to the road. Pulling up the road, David hangs a right and then a left on the road leading to their house. One of the neighbors waters his lawn while he looks up at the Jeep and sees a bright blue sleeping bag fall out of the passenger seat. He watches the Jeep stop, and then back up.

"Get UP. GET UP. GET YOUR FUCKING ASS UP. UP. GET UP," yells David.

Element of Blank

The neighbor watches with curiosity as David gets out of the vehicle and looks down at the sleeping bag, yelling and demanding again for it to rise. Finally, David grabs the object (which the neighbor can now see is too heavy to be a sleeping bag) and pushes it back into the Jeep. Getting into his seat, David slams his hands on the steering wheel, and pops the Jeep into gear, spinning into town in the direction of the hospital.

He walks up to the emergency room, the bundle of Sally in his arms and deposits her onto a stretcher. Half her head smashed, the asphalt having torn it apart at 30 mph, he simply sets her on the stretcher. Without a blink of emotion, or an instant of reflection, he leaves. Her blood drying on his shirt collar and neck and hand, he drives back to their house, fires up his Harley and drives. An hour later, he arrives back at the emergency doors, his Harley parked in the lot, and Sally's blood brown and dry on his neck and shirt. Seeing the woman who met him at the door, David approaches her.

"Where is Sally?"

"Sally...the woman that you brought in?" asks the receptionist incredulously. "She's not alive. She was D.O.A."

"Oh."

Occasionally, on the way to another grave, one of us will pass Sally's plot and pause. No one in town has ever noticed but maybe, in the early morning hours, the mother coyote stands guard over Sally's body, amongst the headstones and tumbleweeds. Much goes unobserved; one can never tell. David has returned to being a motorcycle cowboy. Apparently, based on the eyewitness accounts and the coroner's report, David wasn't responsible for Sally's death. The bruises on her face, they could tell were from David's hand, but his hands, they say, didn't kill her. In a sense, she killed herself, colliding in her lucid state against the moving asphalt. Her girls live with their aunt now. And no one knows how they are because the aunt doesn't live here. The only piece of that family that's still here are Sally's parts...the flesh, the bones, the postmortem hair and nails slowly growing inside her coffin, next to her crushed cheek bone. Slowly, her memory becomes distant, and the children forget who she was. Adults and elders let her memory fade gently up into the vagueness of smoke, and the void that her magic once filled slowly plugs up with desert sand.

www.ingramcontent.com/pod-product-compliance
Lightning Source LLC
Chambersburg PA
CBHW031203020726
47499CB00002B/462